THE DRAGON SCORNED

DARK WORLD: THE DRAGON TWINS 3

MICHELLE MADOW

DREAMSCAPE PUBLISHING

1

GEMMA

Genevieve leaned over an atlas in the tearoom in the Haven, a pendulum in one hand and one of Mira's favorite sandals in the other. The sandals were one of the few things Mira had in her room in the Haven from our old life, since she'd been wearing them when we'd left home for Utopia.

She'd saved up money for *months* to buy those sandals. They were by some fancy designer, so they cost hundreds of dollars.

It was ridiculous.

Then again, I spent most of my money on hardcover books to display on my shelves instead of buying them as ebooks. So who was I to judge?

Genevieve stared at the pendulum's crystal, putting all of her concentration into the spell.

It refused to move.

Mary, Queen Katherine, Ethan, my mom, the vampire prophetess Constance, and the dragon shifter Isemay watched from the sides. All of them were quiet.

After a few minutes of trying, Genevieve placed the pendulum down on the atlas, and the sandal on the table next to it. "It's not working." She looked at me, her eyes full of apology. "I'm sorry."

"You're the most powerful witch in the world," I said. "How is it *not working?*"

Mira wore a cloaking ring, like the rest of us. But Genevieve thought she'd be able to get past its magic without a problem. She was, after all, an ancestor of Geneva—a witch who'd had magic beyond what should have been possible. If anyone could track down Mira, it was Genevieve.

"Wherever Mira is, she's hidden by magic that I can't get through," she said. "I'm truly sorry. I wish I could have helped."

Ethan walked up to me and wrapped his arms around me.

I shrugged him off. Because if it hadn't been for the secrets he'd kept—mainly, that he loved me instead of Mira—then my twin never would have run off and gone missing in the first place.

After I'd returned to consciousness—Mira had hit me *hard* with her magic, which had put me out for a few hours—we'd left the Seventh Kingdom for the Haven. Everything had been so hurried since getting back that we hadn't told my mom and Mary anything other than that Mira was missing, and that we had to find her.

Now, Mary watched us expectantly. "You clearly have a lot to fill us in on," she said. "But first, I believe introductions should be made."

"Of course." Queen Katherine stepped forward. "I'm Katherine—the Queen of the Seventh Kingdom."

Mary's eyes hardened. "The Seventh Kingdom doesn't exist."

"While small, the Seventh Kingdom does, in fact, exist," Katherine said.

"All of the kingdoms are ruled by an original vampire. Well, *were* ruled by an original vampire," Mary corrected herself, since King Alexander—a vampire who'd been turned by Queen Laila—reigned the Vale after Queen Laila's death. "I know all of the original vampires. You're not one of them."

"I am one of them," Queen Katherine said. "You and I used to be friends."

"You and I have never met."

"You don't remember my existence because I'm

gifted with amplified compulsion," Katherine explained what she'd already told me, Ethan, and Mira back in the Seventh Kingdom. "I made you—and all others who knew me—forget about my existence. Then I went with Genevieve, Constance, and Isemay to a small island off the Antarctic Peninsula, where we've guarded the Holy Crown ever since."

All was silent as Mary took it in.

"It sounds like we need to sit down," she finally said. "Because if what you're saying is true, then we're going to be here for a while."

We had breakfast as we filled Mary and Mom in on everything that had happened since we'd left for Antarctica.

"No wonder Mira took off the way she did." Mom glared at Ethan. "You *used* her. And for her to find out like that..." She shook her head, as if unable to find the words. "You broke her heart."

She didn't even look at me.

Did she *blame* me?

"I didn't know," I said quickly. "I was just as surprised as Mira when Ethan put the Crown on my head."

"I didn't want you to find out like that," Ethan said. "*Either* of you."

"One moment." Mary held up a hand, quieting us. "I think we should discuss the Crown's magic. The fifth element."

"Time travel," I said, amazed that it was possible.

"You're *positive* you traveled through time? You didn't teleport to the other room and experience an intense dream while there?"

"I'm positive," I said.

"Then prove it."

"How?"

"Five minutes before you all arrived here, I was sitting down for breakfast in my house," she said. "Go back to that moment and give me this." She pulled a ring off her middle finger and handed it to me.

It was the triple moon, with a moonstone in the center. Eight diamonds surrounded it, and it was set in gold. I couldn't imagine how expensive it must have been.

"Every gemstone is unique," Mary said. "I'll know this one is mine—especially when directly comparing it to itself."

"I've only traveled back in time once," I said. "I'm not exactly sure how it works…"

Mid-sentence, I realized that wasn't correct. Because

when I'd traveled back in time, I'd been wondering what Ethan's expression had looked like when he'd crowned me instead of Mira.

The Crown was connected to my soul. I was the Queen of Pentacles—I *commanded* the Holy Crown. It would bring me to whenever I told it to take me.

"Never mind," I said. "I think I can do it."

"Then do it," Mary said. "I'll see you soon."

I closed my eyes and focused on the Crown sitting on my head.

It warmed, like it was listening to me.

Take me to Mary's house, I thought. *Five minutes before we arrived at the Haven.*

Magic burst through me. Thankfully, it wasn't painful, like the first time I'd traveled through time. It was like a cord had released me from the physical world and was bringing me somewhere else.

Unlike teleporting, it didn't happen instantaneously. I flickered a few times, then broke free of the physical world and floated around like a cloud.

I turned solid again, and I opened my eyes.

I was sitting in the same spot, on a bench in the Haven's tearoom.

But now, the room was empty.

I looked at the clock on the wall and gasped.

It had worked. Well, partly. I hadn't teleported to

Mary's house, but I'd traveled back in time to five minutes before we'd arrived at the Haven.

Which meant I had five minutes to get to Mary's house and tell her about our impending arrival. No big deal, thanks to the magical key Hecate had given me the first time I'd visited her Eternal Library.

I used the key in the door to the tearoom and stepped into the ivory entry hall of the Eternal Library. The tall, arched ceilings and marble floors stretched out to the double door entrance that led to endless bookshelves full of everything you could ever want to know.

The books had no titles, and no way to search through them. The only person who could locate the book with the information you desired was the goddess of witchcraft, Hecate.

The goddess rarely waited in the ivory hall, and today proved no different.

Not like it mattered, since I wasn't there for information. I was there to take advantage of the other handy trick of the key—its ability to let me leave the Library and walk through the door of any place I'd ever been.

Today's destination?

Mary's house. Not a far journey, since it was across the kingdom, but the key made it faster. Plus, this way I wouldn't risk being stopped by residents of the Haven, which would be bound to happen, given that I was wearing the Holy Crown on my head.

I stepped back through the door, into the main living space of Mary's house.

The Haven's mantra was equality for all. So, like all of its houses for a single person or a couple, Mary's was the size of a one-bedroom apartment.

Just like she'd said, she was in the kitchen, bringing her breakfast and a glass of blood to the table.

Surprise crossed her face, and she set her food and drink down, her gaze focused on the top of my head.

"You found the Holy Crown," she said steadily. "And you're—"

"The Queen of Pentacles," I interrupted, since we had limited time. "It's a long story, but you'll understand everything soon. Right now, I'm here to give you this."

I walked forward and handed her the ring.

She studied it, confused, and compared it to the identical ring on her finger.

I said nothing as I waited for her to put it together.

"Where did you get this?" she finally asked.

"It's yours. You gave it to me," I said. "Well, you're *going* to give it to me."

She continued to look back and forth between the rings, searching for a difference between them. "It's exactly the same, down to the smallest details," she said, and she looked back up at me, her eyes full of questions. "This isn't possible."

"Put it in your pocket for now," I said quickly. "I'm going to arrive in the tearoom with Ethan and some others in about four minutes. When I do, don't mention that I was here."

She did as I requested and pocketed the ring. "Why don't you sit down," she said calmly, and she gestured to the table. "It sounds like we have a lot to discuss."

"Wait to give the ring to me until I say how surprised I was when Ethan put the Crown on my head," I continued, ignoring her invitation to join her for breakfast. "I'm sorry for being so vague, but I promise it won't be long until this all makes sense."

I focused on the Crown's magic and thought, *Take me back to the present.* And *to the tearoom.*

I flickered out and re-appeared in the same place in Mary's kitchen.

Mary was no longer there.

The digital clock on her oven showed it was the same time it had been when I'd left.

Suddenly, two memories overlapped in my mind.

The first was the one that had originally happened— Mary's expression of shock and disbelief when I'd told her that the Crown allowed me to travel through time.

In the second memory, Mary's lips had opened into

an O of understanding, and her hand had gone to her pocket where she'd been keeping the ring. Instead of asking me if I was positive I'd traveled through time, she'd calmly handed me the ring and asked me to go back to when she was having breakfast and to give it to her, so I could prove my ability was real.

The second memory—the one of the new reality—layered over the first. The first memory—the one of the reality I'd changed—was still there, although it didn't feel *solid* like the second one.

By giving Mary the ring, I'd erased the timeline where she'd been shocked to learn that the fifth element was time travel and replaced it with a timeline where my visit to give her the ring had clicked into place in her mind.

Kind of confusing, but also pretty cool.

I used the key to return to the tearoom, and Mary's lips curved into a knowing smile.

She pulled the ring out of her pocket and slipped it back onto her finger. "You should have gone back an hour earlier and explained what was going on," she said. "It would have saved me a lot of confusion."

"I wasn't the one who decided to go back five minutes," I said. "It was *your* idea."

She frowned, as if disappointed in her other self's time travel logic. "In the Seventh Kingdom, you teleported to the other room," she said, changing the subject. "So why didn't you teleport into my house instead of going through the Library?"

"I tried." I shrugged. "It didn't work."

She made a sound of disapproval.

"So you walked to Mary's house?" my mom asked. "Did anyone see you wearing the Crown?"

"I went through the Eternal Library."

"You found the nearest witch and got her to teleport you," my mom said, as if she hadn't heard me. "Smart."

"Yep." I nodded, pretending that was exactly what I'd said.

Thanks to Hecate's magic, the only people who knew about the Eternal Library's existence were ones who'd been given keys. Which meant that when someone without a key heard anything about the Eternal Library, their minds replaced what they'd heard with something that made sense to them.

"Very smart," Mary said. "Now, go back again."

"What?" I asked, since I'd already proven that I could travel through time. "Why?"

"I'm curious to see if you can rewrite history again. This time, give me two rings." She removed the moonstone ring again, plus the opal ring next to it, and handed both to me.

"They'll be two of me there," I said. "And three moonstone rings."

I studied the ring in my hand. What would happen when it got back to the present? Would there be *two* of the same ring, since I'd have gone back in time twice? Or would I somehow cancel out the other version of myself—and the other version of the ring? Could I keep going back to the same point in time and change it until getting the result I wanted?

"Couldn't this cause some sort of paradox?" Ethan asked, bringing me out of my confusing, looping thoughts.

"The Crown is a Holy Object," Mary said. "It won't harm itself. And to use it the best we can, we need to learn how it works."

"We can learn how it works later," I said. "Right now, we need to keep searching for Mira."

Genevieve smirked. "You're awfully focused on the present for someone who can travel through time."

I glared at her, then refocused on Mary. "We're finding Mira."

"This will only take a minute," she said. "Satisfy my curiosity, and then I'll help you search for Mira for the rest of the day."

"Thank you."

"But tomorrow, we learn more about the Crown. Deal?"

"Deal," I said, since tomorrow, I intended for Mira to be back in the Haven with us.

So, eager to get it over with, I closed my eyes and asked the Crown to take me back to five minutes before I arrived in the Haven—again.

2

GEMMA

"It isn't working."

I re-opened my eyes, and unsurprisingly, they were all still there watching me. The time on the clock hadn't changed.

"So you can't go back to a time you've already visited," Mary said. "Good to know."

"That seems to be the case." I was unsure if this was a good thing or a bad thing. Probably a bad thing, because it meant that once I went back in time and changed something, I had no do-overs. At least, not from that same point in time. "Now, let's get back to finding Mira. Because I have an idea about where to start."

I told them my idea, and they agreed it was worth a try. Well, *Mary* agreed it was worth a try. Hecate's magic made the others go along with agreeing it was a good idea, despite their obvious confusion.

"I'm coming with you," Ethan said.

I spun around and glared at him. "No."

He stood strong, apparently unaffected by my refusal. "I don't want you going alone."

"I'll be perfectly safe there. Besides, it's not like you can travel with me."

Mary's interest perked up. "That's something we need to test," she said.

"What is?" I asked.

"If you can bring anyone back in time with you or not."

"We'll test it once I'm back," I said, since she was right—it *was* something we needed to know. "Right now, I'm getting my sister."

"You know she might not want to go anywhere with you," Ethan said.

I raised an eyebrow. "And you think it would help if *you* were there?"

"Maybe."

"Wrong. She hates you after what you did."

She hates me, too.

Grief swelled within me, and I tried my best to swallow it down. Because Mira *couldn't* hate me. She was my twin. She could be angry at me—and we'd certainly had our fair share of fights. But she'd never hate me.

She'd also never said she hated me, no matter how bad our fights had been.

She was never going to forgive me for this.

Did I even deserve her forgiveness?

I pushed the thought away. I'd worry about it later. Now, I only had one mission—getting Mira back.

And so, I walked up to the door, put my key in the lock, and returned to Hecate's Eternal Library.

I breathed easier once I was there. Something about the Library was so soothing. It had to be Hecate's magic that filled the air.

The calmness didn't last long, because a second later, Ethan walked through the door.

I stepped back. "I told you not to follow me."

"And I didn't listen."

"Clearly." I crossed my arms, having nothing more to say to him.

"Gemma." His voice was pained as he said my name. "I didn't want you to find out like this."

"You led Mira on for months. You acted like I didn't exist. What the hell was going through your mind?"

"It's complicated." He blew out a long breath and ran a hand through his hair in frustration. "I was confused—until the first time I shifted on Ember."

"The moment dragons know if they have a twin flame."

"How did you know that?" He tilted his head, searching my eyes for answers.

Because another version of you told me in a dream. Or a hallucination. In whatever it was that had happened when I'd been drugged by the nightshade.

At the same time, my heart leaped. Because he'd basically confirmed that he was my twin flame. The connection I felt with him wasn't one sided.

He loved me. And I loved him.

But right now, I was *pissed* at him.

"It's complicated," I said instead. "But we don't have time for this right now. I need to find Mira."

I closed my eyes and focused on the Crown's magic, searching for it in my soul like I had the other times I'd used it.

Nothing was there.

I dug deeper.

Still, nothing.

Take me to the moment Mira left the Seventh Kingdom, I thought, despite the fact that the magic wasn't answering my call.

I opened my eyes, and Ethan was still there, watching me.

"Well?" he asked.

"My magic's gone." I touched the Crown, making sure it was still there despite feeling its weight on my head. "Something's wrong."

"Your magic isn't gone," he said. "At least, not forever."

"What do you mean?"

"We're in Hecate's realm," he said. "And in Hecate's realm—"

"She blocks all magic that isn't witch magic," I finished his sentence, feeling stupid for not putting it together myself. "The Crown's magic isn't witch magic. Time travel is the fifth element. And elemental magic is *dragon* magic."

"Yep." He nodded.

"I can't time travel here." I cursed, since I'd really believed my plan was going to work. "So there's no point in staying here. Let's go back."

"Wait."

I spun around and glared at him again. "What?"

"I'm sorry."

I shook my head, turned away from him, and walked to the door. The sight of him made me feel sick. I couldn't look at him. Not without Mira's final words echoing in my head.

I hate you.

I needed her to understand that none of this was my fault. I needed her forgiveness.

To do that, I needed to find her. I was *going* to find her.

And I refused to let my feelings for Ethan distract me from getting my sister back.

3

GEMMA

"We should send a witch to check in on the café," Mom said once Ethan and I were back. "Mira would have needed comfort. She would have wanted to go *home*."

I nodded, since Mom was right. I'd been feeling at home in the supernatural world, but Mira missed our old life and had been plagued with homesickness daily.

"If Mira had gone to the café, Shivani would have told us," Mary said gently.

"Just satisfy me and send someone to check," Mom said.

"I'll go," I volunteered.

"You'll stay right here," Mary said. "Lilith and her dark witches know where you lived. It's not safe for you to go there."

"I won't be there for long."

"Perhaps. But you're a Queen now. You can't risk yourself when there are pawns lined up and ready to put themselves in the line of fire for you."

I glanced down at the floor, deciding this wasn't a good time to admit that I'd already gone back to the café —when Shivani had brewed that memory potion for me.

I looked at the door, half ready to march toward it and go anyway.

Mom spoke before I had a chance. "The first person who talks to Mira should be me," she said. "I'll go with the witch."

"Bad idea," Mary said. "If there are demons watching the café, there's a chance they'll know who you are. We can't risk them seeing you and taking you as bait to lure the twins back to Lilith's lair."

"So I'll take invisibility potion," she said. "With the potion plus my cloaking ring, they'll have no idea I'm there."

Mary looked at me. "What are your thoughts on this?"

"Mom should go," I said. "If there's anyone Mira will listen to, it's her."

It was true, although I hated the fact that I might be sending my mom somewhere dangerous, especially since she had practically no magic.

But the café wasn't dangerous. I'd been there recently, and I'd been fine.

"If Mira isn't there, you'll come right back," I told her.

"Of course."

Mary reached for the pen and paper on the coffee table, wrote a quick message, then looked at me. "Take the Crown off and hide it behind a pillow," she said.

"Why?"

"Because I'm sending for a witch to come here and take your mom to the café, and I don't want her asking any questions. There's a time for others to learn that you're the Queen of Pentacles, and this isn't it."

I removed the Crown and placed it behind the decorative pillow next to me. I kept my hand resting on the pillow, protecting it.

Mary had Genevieve send the fire message, and two minutes later, a witch named Riya teleported into the tearoom with two vials of invisibility potion. I'd had lunch with her a few times when I'd been training in the Haven—she'd always been warm and welcoming.

Mary quickly briefed her on the mission.

"Got it," Riya said, then she took a deep breath and asked, "Has there been any word on Queen Elizabeth?"

The Queen of Utopia hadn't been seen since the demons and dark witches had plundered her kingdom, destroying it and killing everyone there. She'd stayed behind to fight and hadn't been heard from since. We all hoped for the best, but the longer she was gone, the more dire her situation seemed to be.

"The Nephilim army is working hard to locate her," Mary said.

"And we're working on locating my daughter," Mom said to Riya. "Are you ready?"

Riya nodded, then she and Mom drank the invisibility potion and disappeared.

"I'm taking her now." Riya's voice came from where she'd been standing, even though I couldn't see her. "Be back soon."

A few seconds passed.

"Did you leave?" I asked.

No one replied, which I took as a yes.

"While we wait for them to return, we might as well make good use of time," Mary said to me. "Let's do more tests."

From her stoic expression, I could tell she thought I was going to refuse.

"All right," I said, since I was as eager to learn more about my new magic as anyone. And with Mom and Riya at the café looking for Mira, studying my magic was the best thing I could do to help find my twin. "I'm guessing you already know what you want me to try next?"

"We need to figure out if you can take anyone with you when you travel," she said. "Also, I'm curious if you can go to the future as well as the past."

"Let's try that first," I said quickly. "The future one."

She had a good point about needing to see if I could bring anyone with me when I traveled. But what if I hurt them in the process?

What if I hurt *him?*

I glanced at Ethan, since I knew he'd insist on being my test subject.

From the hard determination in his eyes, I was right.

"I'll go a minute into the future," I said, since they did that in one of my favorite movies, *Back to the Future*. "I'll reappear for you in a minute. For me, it'll be like I never left."

I closed my eyes and pulled at the magic inside the Crown.

Unlike in Hecate's realm, its warmth filled me, answering my call.

Take me a minute into the future, I told it.

The magic slipped out of my grasp, then faded away.

I tried again. And again. And again.

Each time, the magic disappeared.

I opened my eyes and looked at everyone in the

room except for Ethan. If I pretended he wasn't there, I could pretend my feelings for him weren't there, too.

"I can't travel into the future," I said, and then I looked at Constance. "But you already knew that, right? Since you can see the future."

"I see the future as it will play out without my interference," she said. "If I intervene, I see the new future I've created, along with the one that would have originally existed. I also see the future without your interference, as your magic seems to exist outside the realm of my visions."

"But you knew I was there in the Seventh Kingdom, right? When I was in the bedroom, and the other version of myself heard me move around?"

"The moment you appeared in the bedroom, the future I saw changed."

"And you stopped the other version of me from seeing myself."

"I stopped the other version of you from investigating the room where you were hiding," she said. "I was keeping the original future—the one where Ethan crowned you uninterrupted—intact."

"So you remember *both* possible futures?"

"Yes."

"Interesting," I said, even though it was making my head spin.

"Confusing," Genevieve muttered.

Queen Katherine remained silent, taking it all in.

"It will get less confusing once we do more tests," Mary said. "Take me three minutes into the past."

"Why three?" I asked.

"It's the lucky number of witchcraft."

I stood up to walk toward her, relieved to be taking her instead of Ethan.

"Wait." Ethan stood up as well, and my heart dropped, because I knew what was coming. "Take me. After all, we shouldn't risk a queen when there's a pawn to offer himself up in the line of duty."

"You're not a pawn," I shot back. "You're the King of Ember."

"And it's my job to protect you. I can't do that if you're alone in the past."

"I won't be alone," I said. "The past version of you will be there."

"Which brings up another question," Mary said. "What happens when the past version of you sees the future version?"

"I wouldn't know," I said. "I watched the past version of myself in the Seventh Kingdom, but she didn't see me."

"It's another test to conduct," Mary said.

"It is," I agreed. "But first, you wanted to see if I can

bring anyone with me." I turned to face Genevieve, Constance, and Isemay. "You're the only three in here who aren't rulers of a kingdom. Do one of you want to try to travel back in time with me?"

Constance lowered her gaze, like I used to do in lower school when I didn't want to get called on to answer a question.

I took that as a no.

Genevieve stood up and straightened out her white tunic. The gear we'd worn in Antarctica was stifling in the Haven, so while we'd filled Mary in on what had happened in the Seventh Kingdom, she'd sent for Haven whites for us to change into.

"I'll do it," she said. "I'm always down for an adventure."

"Three minutes into the past is hardly an adventure," I said with a small smile. "But thank you for volunteering."

"I'm the most powerful witch in the world," she said. "A little bit of time travel won't kill me."

I nodded, took her hands, then called on the Crown's magic.

Take us three minutes into the past.

The magic filled me, flowed into Genevieve, and we flickered out.

We solidified less than a second later. Genevieve's

hands were still firmly in mine, and I opened my eyes, relieved to find her fully intact.

But we weren't in the tearoom.

We were in the hall outside of it.

The door was closed, but if we were three minutes in the past like we were supposed to be, the other versions of ourselves were on the other side.

"Are you okay?" I asked Genevieve, since the first time I'd time traveled had been agonizing.

"That felt more... turbulent than teleporting." She smiled mischievously. "It was fun."

"So it didn't hurt?"

"Not at all."

The pain that first time must have been from receiving my magic—not from the experience of time traveling for the first time.

Good. I hated to think I'd ever have to put anyone in that much pain.

It was also interesting that the two times I'd traveled back to a place I'd been, I'd appeared in the nearest room, where the past version of me couldn't see the current version of me. The two other times, I hadn't moved.

The Crown apparently didn't want me materializing in front of my past self.

But I wondered...

"What would happen if we went inside?" I tilted my head toward the door leading into the tearoom.

"We'd come face to face with our past selves," she said.

"And what would happen when they saw us?"

She raised an eyebrow. "You're the one with time travel magic. What do *you* think will happen when they see us?"

She spoke as if we were definitely going to do it.

"I don't know." I shrugged, then tried to think of the worst possible scenario. "We could cause a paradox, and the world could implode?"

Her expression turned serious. "Then it sounds like we shouldn't open that door."

"I wasn't being serious," I said. "Well, I suppose the paradox is a possibility. But I don't think I would have been given the Holy Crown if I was going to implode the world from opening a door."

"Agreed," she said. "So, what do you want to do?"

"We're here to test out my magic." I moved closer to the door. "So, let's test it."

4

GEMMA

Genevieve stood behind me as I reached for the door, leaving practically no space between the two of us. She was taller than me, so she could get a good view of what was happening by watching over my head. We were like children trying to eavesdrop on the adults after bedtime.

I held the doorknob, then paused.

"Are you going to do it?" she whispered. "Or do you need me to?"

"I can do it."

Not wanting to give myself a chance to hesitate—and also, because our three minutes would be up soon—I twisted the handle and pulled the door open.

My eyes met Constance's, then Isemay's… and then I flickered out.

When I reappeared, the time on the clock was the same as it had been when I'd left.

New memories layered on top of the old ones.

"I won't be alone," I told Ethan. "The past version of yourself will be there."

Suddenly, the door opened. I looked to see who was there, but the space was empty.

Embers glowed in Ethan's palms, and he stood ready to attack.

"Relax," Constance said. "Everything's fine."

Ethan stepped out into the hall, checked out both directions, then came back inside. "Unless there are ghosts in the Haven, then someone took invisibility potion and is in here with us." He looked around the room in suspicion. "Show yourself."

"No one's here." Constance was as calm as ever.

"Then who opened the door?"

"Gemma and Genevieve," she said. "I saw both of you for a moment, then you flickered out."

"I saw the both of you, too," Isemay said.

"I saw nothing," said Genevieve. She was sitting next to Isemay, which meant she would have been the next person in the room who would have gotten a look at our mysterious visitors.

"You flickered out a split second after I saw you," Isemay said.

"Flickered out," I repeated. "We time traveled. Together."

Mary smiled. "Then it appears that yes, you can bring someone with you," she said. "I was about to ask what happens when a past version of yourself sees a future version of yourself, but it looks like we just got an answer."

"We disappeared right before we could see the future versions of ourselves," I said. "The question is—where did we go? And **when** *did we go?"*

"There's only one way to find out," she said, and just like the first time, Genevieve and I traveled three minutes into the past.

We didn't have the conversation about possible paradoxes. I didn't hesitate before opening the door. Instead, I opened it confidently and was forced back into the present right before we would have seen ourselves, appearing exactly where we were right now.

In the present, a second after we'd left.

I stepped through the door, Genevieve right behind me.

Ethan rushed over to make sure I was okay, but I brushed him off and faced Mary. "Time won't let our past selves see our current selves," I said. "Right before it would have happened, we were forced back into the present."

I continued on to tell them about how the two memories had layered on top of each other and that I could differentiate between which one was the original timeline, and which was the altered, current timeline.

Genevieve had memories of both timelines as well.

"This all leads us to a new question," Mary said. "Can you bring *two* people with you?"

"There's only one way to find out," I said, and I turned to Isemay. "Do you want to try to tag along with me and Genevieve?"

Ethan stepped in front of her before she could answer and faced me. "We know you can travel with someone else without harming them," he said carefully, like he was gearing up for me to reject whatever he was about to propose. "I'll travel with you and Genevieve."

"Fine," I said, since Genevieve would be with us, which meant Ethan wouldn't be able to corner me into having a conversation with him that I wasn't emotionally ready to have until I knew Mira wasn't in danger.

He relaxed, the relief clear on his face.

I held out both my hands. Genevieve took one, and Ethan took the other.

Ethan's palm radiated warmth, and it flowed through my arm and into my core. My cheeks flushed as desire hot as fire shot through me, like a flame connecting us together.

No, I told myself, trying to ground myself in the

earth to cool the fire. *Don't get distracted from finding Mira.*

I closed my eyes and told the Crown to take us six minutes into the past.

The Crown's magic pulled back, like it was telling me no.

"It's not working." I pulled my hands out of theirs, although the warmth from Ethan's remained. I rubbed my palm against my pants, as if they could absorb the heat. They couldn't. "It seems like I can only take one person back at a time."

Mary nodded, easily accepting this. "Another thought," she said. "What happens if—"

She didn't get a chance to finish, because Riya and Mom teleported back into the tearoom.

Mom's hair was up in a knot on the top of the head, like she always put it when she was frazzled and trying to focus, and her breaths were short, as if she'd been running around.

My heart sank at the panic in her eyes. "What happened?"

"They weren't there," she said. "*Either* of them. I tried to send Shivani a fire message, but it didn't go through."

Grief washed over me. Because if a fire message wasn't going through, it meant one of two things.

Either Shivani was being kept prisoner somewhere,

or she was dead.

"We searched every inch of the place for clues," Riya continued, although it was evident from her tone that a possible clue she was searching for was Shivani's dead body. "There was nothing. And nothing was out of place. Whatever happened to her, there was no struggle. And there was one more thing." She turned to me, took a deep breath, and said, "Mira's scent was fresh in her room."

I swallowed. "How fresh?"

"Fresh enough that it seems likely she went there immediately after leaving the Seventh Kingdom."

"I'm going." I reached for my key and headed toward the door.

Ethan was by my side in an instant. "You're not going alone."

Mom sat on the couch, her expression blank, like she was in shock. "You won't find anything," she said. "We checked everywhere."

"You're not thinking fourth dimensionally," I said.

She snapped her head up. "What do you mean?"

"Time," I said, and I touched the Crown to show what I meant. "I'm not going to look for Mira in the present. I'm going to go back in time to the moment she stepped through that door, so I'm there when she arrives."

5

GEMMA

"Good plan." Mom stood up. "I'm going with you."

"No," Ethan said.

"Yes." Mom didn't budge. "Mira will want to see *me*. Not you."

"Mira was out of control," he said calmly. "We don't know how dangerous she might be. I need to go with Gemma, as backup."

"Backup for what?"

"Backup in case she attacks."

"She'd never attack me. I'm her mother." Mom looked at me, like she was waiting for me to take her side.

I wished I could.

"She attacked me," I said slowly. "Back in the Seventh Kingdom. She threw me against that wall so hard that it knocked me out. And we'll be going back to *immediately* after that moment. Ethan's right. We have no idea how dangerous she might be."

"She was angry with you," Mom said. "She wouldn't have actually hurt you."

"Except she *did* actually hurt me." I couldn't believe it was true, but I'd seen the enraged look in Mira's eyes when she'd thrown her magic at me. She was capable of far more than I'd ever given her credit for.

If she lost control and hurt Mom, I'd never be able to forgive myself.

"She was volatile," I said. "Ethan and I will be prepared and can fight back with our magic. You have practically no magic. If she attacks, you won't be able to defend yourself."

"And what if she leaves? You have no idea where she'll go next."

"She won't be able to leave," Ethan said. "I'll block the door."

It made perfect sense to *me*, since Mira couldn't travel through the Eternal Library if she couldn't use her key in the door. But Mom nodded, as if it made sense to her, too.

"She's my twin," I continued, my voice softer. "I love her, too. I'm going to bring her back to us."

Even if that means fighting her with my magic and forcing her through that door.

Mom said nothing, and I worried she was going to keep arguing with me on this.

"All right," she gave in. "Just make sure to bring her straight back."

"I will," I said. "I promise."

I gave her a hug, then walked through the door and into the Eternal Library. Ethan followed me, but I didn't pause in the Library's ivory hall—I didn't want to give him the opportunity to pull me into a conversation about *us*.

Whatever *we* were.

I stepped into Mira's bedroom, and he followed right behind me.

Like always, I was greeted by Mira's giant shoe rack, where she displayed them all like treasures. It was like a bookcase, but for shoes.

Her window was open, letting in the salty smell of the ocean. And the scent of the ocean was mixed with the warm, spicy one of cinnamon buns.

Mira's scent.

Like Riya had said, it was fresh. So fresh that it was like my sister could be right downstairs.

Even though Mom and Riya had already checked the apartment and café, I raced through the entire place to do the same. The sign on the door was set to closed, and everything was where it should have been. Shivani had been taking perfect care of our home, which I already knew, since I'd been there a few weeks ago.

I raced through as I checked every room, not giving Ethan the opportunity to start a conversation. Once finished checking the basement, I hurried back up to Mira's room.

Ethan followed, not saying a word. At least he was respecting the fact that I didn't want to talk.

He watched me from the center of the room. "What's the plan?" he asked.

"We'll stand in front of the door when we travel back to the past, so we're already blocking it when we arrive. And then..." I frowned, since I didn't want to hurt Mira. "We'll be catching her by surprise. Maybe she'll talk to us."

It was a terrible "plan," and we both knew it.

"We'll see what she's like when she arrives," he said. "If she's out of control, we'll use this." He reached into his pocket and pulled out a dart full of deep blue potion.

Complacent potion.

"Where'd you get that?" I asked.

"Genevieve gave it to me when you were unconscious. She said I'd know when to use it."

Of course she did. Complacent potion was one of the

—if not *the*—most difficult potion to brew. Most of the high witches of the kingdom couldn't even create it. It was also highly illegal, although law had sort of gone out the window, given the war with the demons and everything.

I wanted to say that I'd never drug my twin.

But she'd thrown me against a wall so hard that she'd knocked me out. And if this was what it took to get her to the Haven, then so be it.

"Because of my air magic, my aim is flawless." He put it back inside his pocket. "Once we're in the room with her, I'll shoot her with the potion dart."

"You'll shoot her with it *if* she attacks," I said before he could continue. "If she's willing to talk to us, we don't drug her."

"Deal. Then you'll grab her, take her to the present, and get her to the Haven. Once she's back safely, you can return to the moment you left and get me. It'll be like no time passed for me."

"You sure know a lot about time travel," I said.

"I've seen *Back to the Future* a few times," he said. "Great movie. And *Prisoner of Azkaban* was one of my favorites in the Harry Potter series. That was the one with the—"

"Time turner," I finished for him. "It was one of my favorites, too. Along with *Goblet of Fire*."

He gave me a small smile, and for a moment it felt like everything was normal, and we were just two people spending time together, talking about books and movies.

I wanted to grab his hand and pull him into my room so I could show him my bookshelf. There were a bunch of other books there that he'd read and loved, too. And while the Ethan from my nightshade memories had seen it, the *real* Ethan—the one who was in front of me right now—hadn't.

"Wait," I said, the thought of my room making me think of something.

"What?"

"Maybe we shouldn't appear immediately in Mira's room."

"Why not?"

"Firstly, because we don't want to startle her," I said. "But mainly because she's angry because you crowned me instead of her. It might not be a good idea for me to be wearing the Crown when we see her."

"What do you want to do with it? Hold it?" he asked. "She'll still be able to see it."

"I'm going to put it in a bag that I'll be holding," I said. "Remember—Mira came here because she misses her old life. It's a small thing, but if I change into my regular clothes, she might be more willing to talk to us."

"That's fine," he said, and then he stepped to the side, so I could lead us to my room.

This version of Ethan had been in our apartment more times than I could count, but he'd never been in *my* room.

My room was cozier than Mira's—and also messier. Not like I was a slob or anything, but she was beyond meticulous about keeping everything in its place. My backpack was slung over my chair, and my binders and schoolbooks arranged haphazardly on my desk, as if I were rushing to meet the deadline of a project. Which I hadn't been, since we'd been on break when we'd left. I just hadn't totally cleaned up after finals the term before.

Ethan's eyes went straight to my bookshelves.

The urge was strong to walk over there with him and point out my favorites. But I restrained myself.

"I'm going to change," I said. "You can wait out in the hall."

"I'm not leaving you alone," he said. "I'll just turn around in here."

"Nothing's going to happen to me while I change," I snapped, although I immediately felt bad about my harsh tone.

It was just that the thought of Ethan being *right there* while I changed was going to create way more tension than I was ready to deal with.

"Fine," he said. "I'll wait in the hall. But you'll keep your door open."

He stepped out, and I changed into my favorite jeans, a tank top, and a sweatshirt with our school's name on the front—John Astor High. Astor was some super rich American who'd sailed to Australia at the end of his life, and tons of things around here were named after him.

Lastly, I picked the simple brown purse up off my dresser—the one I'd always carried with me. My wallet, keys, and Kindle were inside. The Crown would easily fit in there, too, although I obviously needed to keep it on until we arrived in the past.

I studied myself in the mirror, surprised by how *normal* I looked.

I was also surprised that although I should have been at home in my room, I felt out of place. Like I'd outgrown it for bigger, better things.

Things like elemental magic, time travel, visiting other realms, and being a Queen... even though I didn't actually feel like a Queen yet.

"All right," I called to Ethan. "I'm ready."

He came back in and paused when he saw me.

Tension crackled in the air between us.

"What?" I asked.

"Nothing. It's just, you look so... normal."

"That's the goal," I said, trying not to pay attention to the fact that I'd just been thinking the same thing. "Now, are you ready to get this over with?"

"Let's do it."

With that, I walked over to him, took his hands in mine, and told the Crown to bring us back to the moment after Mira had left the Seventh Kingdom.

6

GEMMA

WHEN WE REAPPEARED in my room, everything was the same... except Mira was standing in front of my bookshelf, next to my bed. She was in her Antarctica gear, just like she'd been when she'd left the Seventh Kingdom.

But the rage in her eyes was gone. In fact, when she saw us, she gave us a small smile, like she'd been expecting us. And there was something different about her eyes.

They were a darker blue than usual.

Maybe it had to do with her magic? Were her eyes reflecting the dark emotions inside her?

"Gemma," she said. "Ethan. I knew you'd come after me. How long did it take you to figure out I'd come here?"

I glanced at Ethan's hand. It was near his pocket, but he hadn't reached in for the dart.

"Why are you in my room?" I asked, not bothering to answer her question.

"To snoop around, obviously." She smirked. "To figure out how long the two of you were together behind my back. I figured you'd have written about it in your journal or something."

"My journal's in my suitcase," I said, wondering if our suitcases were still sitting in the living room where we'd left them.

We'd packed as much as possible for Utopia, then learned we weren't allowed to bring our stuff with us. Unless Shivani had moved our bags, they were still in the living room.

"I'll check later." She shrugged, like she didn't care. "Now, back to my question. How long did it take you to figure out that I came straight here?"

Out of all the questions she could have asked us, *that* was what she wanted to know?

It didn't make sense.

"We came from tomorrow," I said.

"Interesting."

She didn't sound interested in the slightest.

She sounded... ambivalent.

Her gaze lifted to right above my head. "Nice crown,"

she said. "It stayed on pretty tightly when you flew through the air. Like it was glued to your head."

"I'm the only one who can take it off," I told her what I'd quickly discovered when I'd woken up in the Seventh Kingdom.

"Convenient."

If she'd asked because she wanted to try to steal it, she seemed unfazed by my answer.

What was going on with her?

I *knew* my twin. And I'd never seen her act so serene and calm. It was eerie, especially given how enraged she'd been when she'd left the Seventh Kingdom.

She'd only arrived moments ago, but I would have expected my room to already look like a tornado had blown through it. Yet, everything was as I'd left it.

"Do you want me to get my journal for you?" I asked. "You can read it. I don't mind."

"No need," she said. "If you'd written anything you didn't want me to see, you wouldn't have offered to hand it over. Anyway," she continued, and she looked to Ethan. "When did you realize you loved Gemma and not me?"

I sucked in a sharp breath, surprised at how nonchalantly she'd said it. And still surprised about how it was *true* that Ethan loved me more than her.

None of it felt real.

"Why don't we go to the Haven and talk about it there?" Ethan said. "Your mom's anxious to see you."

"How would that work, exactly?" She tilted her head, her eyes on my Crown again. "With the time travel and all. Would you bring me there in *this* time? Or would you bring me to the future—to tomorrow, which is your present—and then we'd go to the Haven together?"

I stilled, since I didn't actually know if I could bring someone from the past into the present. I hadn't had time to test it out.

This is why Mary said we needed to do more tests before we left.

Especially since my power technically gave me all the time in the world.

It was going to take me a while to wrap my mind around all this time travel stuff. In the meantime, I was grateful that Mira was cooperating.

Maybe she felt as out of place at home as I did. Maybe coming here made her realize she didn't belong here anymore.

"Mom's already been filled in on everything that happened," I said, not wanting her to know that I wasn't totally sure how the Holy Crown worked. "She's looking forward to seeing you. So I'll bring you to the present—to *my* present. To tomorrow."

Then, once she was back in the Haven, I'd come back and get Ethan.

Our plan was working out way smoother than I'd thought possible.

"Smart choice," she said. "Because given how hard I slammed you into the wall, your past self is currently in the Seventh Kingdom, recovering from that blow to the head. If you brought me to the Haven in *this* time, that means your past self will eventually go there, too. And that would get messy, with having to avoid each other and all of that."

I furrowed my eyebrows, confused. Because Mira didn't read or watch anything with fantasy or science fiction in it. How did she grasp time travel so quickly?

"That's right," I said slowly. "So, does that mean you'll come?"

"No," she said. "You were too late for that."

"What do you mean?"

"I mean that you didn't wake up in time. You see, after a Queen receives her Holy—or Dark—Object, Time writes that moment in stone. Once a Queen, always a Queen. And by the time you were conscious, I'd already been crowned."

She raised her hand and pulled something out of the air next to her shoulder.

A crystal crown.

A crown that matched mine... except its crystals were jet black instead of clear quartz.

The Dark Crown.

She smiled wickedly, then placed the Crown on her head.

By the time Ethan had reached for the dart of complacent potion, she'd already flickered out and disappeared.

7

GEMMA

I RAN to the place where Mira had been standing, as if I could chase her through time.

But I couldn't. Because I had no idea *when* she'd come from. Guessing would be impossible.

"That wasn't Mira," Ethan said slowly, processing what we'd just learned.

I spun around to face him. "It *was* Mira," I said. "But it was a *future* version of Mira. Which means…" I paused and glanced at the door.

"Mira might still be here," he finished my thought.

"The Mira from this present. Before she becomes…" I trailed off again, unable to say it out loud.

"The Dark Queen of Pentacles." It sounded so final when he said it.

"But it hasn't happened yet," I said. "We can stop it before it does. We just have to find her *now*."

I hurried to the door and flung it open, ready to search the entire place for my twin. The first stop? Her bedroom.

She wasn't there… but the warm, spicy smell of chai tea drifted up from the stairwell.

Mira's favorite drink.

I stilled, leaned against the wall, and listened.

Because there were people talking downstairs.

Mira and Shivani.

Ethan stopped walking when he heard them, too.

We listened as Mira talked between sobs, explaining everything that had happened in the Seventh Kingdom to Shivani. She was confessing *everything*.

I pulled Ethan back into Mira's room and quietly shut the door so we could talk freely.

"We'll do the same plan we discussed earlier," I said, being careful to talk softly enough so they wouldn't be able to hear me downstairs.

"What about all the stuff future Mira said?" he asked. "Once a Queen, always a Queen?"

"She went dark—she was probably lying," I said, since I refused to believe anything else. "But *our* Mira is down there right now. We have to save her."

"What about Shivani?"

"We'll save her, too. Demons must have gotten to them. That has to be why they both won't be here tomorrow," I said, easily putting the pieces together in my mind. "But when she sees us, Mira might lose it again. And we don't know when the demons will get here. So the moment she's in eyesight, hit her with that dart. I'll bring her to the future, get her to the Haven, and then I'll come back for you and Shivani."

"If the demons had gotten to them, wouldn't there have been signs of a struggle when your mom and Riya came here to search for them?" Ethan asked.

"Maybe the demons got them quickly," I said. "I don't know. But the longer we stand here talking about it, the more time we lose. Are you in or not?"

"You know I'm in."

"Good."

He took the dart out of his pocket and we tiptoed down the stairs, stopping behind the doorframe when Mira and Shivani came into view.

Mira was holding a cup of chai tea, tears streaming down her face. Shivani sat attentively, listening as Mira vented about what had happened in the Seventh Kingdom.

"He was supposed to crown *me*," Mira said. "He was supposed to love *me*. But no. He picked—"

Ethan shot the dart into the side of her neck before she could finish the sentence.

Her eyes widened in surprise.

Shivani stood and spun around to face the stairs, knocking her chair over. She reached for her dagger, ready to fight.

Ethan and I came down with our hands up to show we weren't going to attack. "It's okay," he said. "We're here to help you."

Shivani wrapped one hand around Mira's arm and used the other to pull a weapon out of the ether.

The Dark Wand.

Steel gray with a ruby crystal on the top, it was the same Wand I'd seen Lavinia use when she'd fought us in Nebraska.

"Too bad I don't want your help." She smirked and shot red magic out of the Wand, toward me and Ethan.

He pulled me down a split second before the magic could hit us, then shot a burst of fire at Shivani.

The fire hit the wall behind where she'd been standing.

Because Shivani and Mira were gone.

Shivani had teleported out with my twin.

I stood there, shocked, watching the wall burn. The flame grew smaller and disappeared, leaving a scorched black circle on the wood.

I wanted to go back and fix it. But I couldn't go back to a time I'd already visited.

"Why did Shivani have the Dark Wand?" I asked instead.

"I don't think that was Shivani," he said.

"What do you mean?"

"I mean that Lavinia would never give up the Dark Wand. Someone would have to kill her and pry it from her hands if they wanted it. And we would have heard if Lavinia was dead."

"So you think that was Lavinia," I said, and he nodded.

I shuddered at the thought of that witch having been in our home.

When I'd come here for the memory potion, had I really been with Shivani? Or had that been Lavinia?

It had to have been Shivani. If it had been Lavinia, she would have taken me, like she'd just taken Mira.

"Lavinia must have gotten to Shivani at some point," he continued. "Used her DNA to make transformation potion so she could take Shivani's place."

"We need to go back in time and stop Lavinia from taking Shivani's place," I said. "If we stop her, she wouldn't have been here today. Then she won't have the chance to take Mira, and Mira won't become the Dark Queen of Pentacles."

"Agreed," he said. "But we shouldn't take on Lavinia alone. We need backup."

"We need the Queen of Swords."

"Exactly. So let's go back to the future, go to the Haven, and get Raven."

I looked around the room—at the fallen chair, the wall scorched by Ethan's fire, and the doorframe that had been cracked by Lavinia's red magic.

If we went back further and stopped Lavinia, then none of this would ever happen.

"Let's do it." I grabbed Ethan's hands, then thought to the Crown, *take us back to the present.*

We flickered out, then reappeared in the present, in the same spot in the café.

Except the scorch mark on the wall was gone. The doorframe was no longer cracked. Mom and Riya could have been the ones who'd picked the chair back up, but there was no way the wall and doorframe could have been fixed that quickly.

The clock on the wall said it was seconds after we'd left.

But what *day* was it?

Unsure how else to check, I hurried up to Mom's office, sat down at her computer, and typed "what day is it" into the Google search bar.

Saturday, March 21. The same day we'd left.

"I don't understand." I sat back and shook my head, trying to make sense of it all.

"I think I do," Ethan said. "Look."

He pulled a dart of complacent potion out of his pocket.

"You had two of them?" I asked.

"I only had one."

"But you used it on Mira."

"I did. But it's back in my pocket, as good as new. Just like the wall and doorframe downstairs are as good as new, too."

"It's like our confrontation with Lavinia and Mira was erased."

"Seems like it."

I shook my head again, not understanding how or why it had happened.

Then the words Dark Mira had said to us replayed in my head, and a sick feeling crept into my stomach.

After a Queen receives her Holy—or Dark—Object, Time writes that moment in stone. Once a Queen, always a Queen.

I reached for the key hanging from my necklace. "Hecate better be in the Library," I said. "Because we need some answers."

8

GEMMA

HECATE MUST HAVE SOMEHOW KNOWN how desperate we were for help, because she was waiting for us in the ivory hall, as serene as ever in her purple gown that reached the floor.

"Gemma," she said. "The Holy Crown looks good on you."

I didn't bother thanking her, or greeting her at all.

"How can I stop Mira from becoming the Dark Queen of Pentacles?" I said instead, getting right to my question.

"Follow me." She spun around and led us into the hall of endless bookshelves.

A woman in a poodle skirt was helping herself to food from the long banquet table in the center—I recognized her from the first time I was in this room. She didn't seem to notice we were there.

Hecate stepped up to the wooden pedestal, and her eyes transformed into galaxies of stars. Smokey, cosmic magic poured out of them and made its way down the hall, tendrils of it breaking off to peruse the books on the shelves. The smoke traveled much farther back than I could see, and it took longer than usual, as if it was reaching deeper than it had for any of my other questions.

Finally, a book flew from the shelves and into Hecate's hands. It was light gray, almost white. And with the book, the mist flew back inside Hecate, and her eyes returned to their normal, deep purple color.

The book opened, and wind blew through the pages, landing on one near the back. As always, Hecate angled the book away from us, so we couldn't read what was inside.

I wondered *why* she wouldn't let us read the books ourselves, but that was a question for another day.

She took a while to read it, looking deep in thought. Finally, she pulled the book closer to her, raised her gaze to look at us, and said, "You cannot stop Mira from becoming the Dark Queen of Pentacles."

I said nothing, waiting for her to continue. Because there had to be more to it than that.

"In the present, Mira has already become the Dark Queen of Pentacles," she said. "Her position as Queen is written in stone—not even Time will allow you to change it. It's the same with all the Queens. If you try to stop them from acquiring the Object that turned them into a Queen, Time will reject the change. The present you return to will be the same one you left, as if you'd never traveled to the past at all."

"Time erased the fact that we went back to help Mira," I realized.

"Yes," she said. "I'm sorry."

Defeat shattered my soul.

My twin was gone. Forever.

But maybe not. Makena—one of the high witches of the Ward—had said that no one but the angels and the demons were truly light or dark. There was light inside of everyone.

Torrence had been able to come back from the dark.

I was going to make sure that Mira would, too.

"Now, Ethan," Hecate said, turning to him. "I take it that you have a question as well?"

"Yes." He stood straighter and kept his eyes locked on Hecate's. "How can I free the dragons from the cuffs that bind their magic?"

"A good question." She faced the shelves, and the cosmic mist floated out of her eyes again.

I wished Ethan had asked more about Mira. He could have thought of *some* question that would help us help her.

But the dragons were his people. He was their king. Freeing them could be the key to defeating the demons.

And if we defeated the demons, maybe we'd have a better chance of helping Mira.

Another book flew into Hecate's hands. This one was such a dark gray that it was nearly black.

Dark magic. I could practically feel the heaviness of it oozing off the pages.

Hecate didn't spend as much time reading the passage inside the book as she had in the one before.

"There's only one way to disable the magic binding cuffs," she said. "You must kill the one who enspelled them."

"Thank you," Ethan said, and we both watched as the books floated off the pedestal, made their way down the hall, and disappeared into its endless shelves.

"Do you know who enspelled the cuffs?" I asked him.

There was no point in asking Hecate—we'd already used up our questions for the day.

"No," he said. "But it's dark mage magic. It has to be one of the dark mages on Ember."

"Got it," I said, and then I turned back to Hecate.

"Thank you," I told her. "For being here when I needed answers the most."

"I'm here for you, always," she said. "Even when I'm not here, in the Eternal Library, my magic is everywhere. To find it, all you have to do is to tune into your intuition."

With that, she disappeared into a cloud of cosmic smoke.

Other than the zombied-out witches roaming the shelves, I was alone with Ethan.

Which meant it was time to get out of there. Because as long as I didn't acknowledge my feelings for him, I didn't have to deal with them.

That was how it worked. Right?

"Come on." I turned my back to Ethan and started to make my way to the ivory hall. "We need to get back to the Haven and tell Mary and the others what we've learned."

9

GEMMA

"Mira was able to pull the Dark Crown out of the ether."

Out of everything we'd told her, *that* was the part of the story Mary cared about the most.

"Yes," I said. "She pulled it out of the ether, told us how we couldn't change the fact that she was a Queen, and traveled back to her present—whenever that might be."

For all we knew, the Mira we'd spoken to in my room could have been a version of her from months from now. Or *years* from now, although she didn't look visibly older than she had the last time I'd seen her.

"It used to be that the only people who could access the ether like that were the chosen champions of Mars," Mary said, referring to the half-blood fae chosen to represent the god of war in the annual Faerie Games held in the Otherworld.

Each god gifted their chosen half-blood with magic unique to them. One of the gifts bestowed by Mars was the ability to access any weapon from the ether.

"The Queen of Wands worked with her soulmate Julian—who was a chosen champion of Mars—to create a spell that allowed people to 'store' a weapon of theirs in the ether," Mary continued. "But as far as I know, Selena was the only one who could cast that spell."

"Lavinia is the Dark Queen of Wands," I said. "She could have worked with a chosen champion of Mars to cast that spell on Mira."

"Exactly what I was thinking," said Mary. "But it's important to note that this is a *spell*. Meaning that Selena didn't use her fae magic to do it. She used her witch magic, which was amplified by the Holy Wand."

"What are you getting at?"

"We have the strongest witch in the world here with us." She looked to Genevieve and asked, "If you worked with a chosen champion of Mars, do you think you could cast a spell that would allow Gemma to store the Holy Crown in the ether?"

"Of course I could." Genevieve straightened her shoulders, like she was offended that Mary would think otherwise. "I might not be the Queen of Wands, but my bloodline has genie magic in it. I can do nearly any type of magic."

Mary's eyes widened. "Genie magic?"

"Yes…" Genevieve looked at her like she had amnesia. Then, she turned to Queen Katherine. "What did you do?"

"Like Mary said, you're the most powerful witch in the world," she said. "Well, you were *one* of the most powerful witches in the world, until your bloodline died out."

Genevieve frowned at the reminder of Geneva's sacrifice.

"If people knew you had genie magic, they'd come looking for you," she continued, but Genevieve interrupted before she could say any more.

"You compelled the world to forget about me."

"Yes."

Genevieve took a moment to soak this in. She didn't seem happy about it, but she wasn't raging with anger, either.

"What's done is done," Katherine said.

"It is," Mary agreed. "So, are you willing to attempt this spell?"

"Hold up," Ethan said. "You're asking her to experiment on Gemma."

"The Crown isn't exactly inconspicuous," Mary said.

"It's too big to keep in anything but a large bag, and a bag can be easily stolen. This is a good solution to that problem."

Silence descended as they looked at me and Genevieve.

From Ethan's expression, I could tell he wanted me to say no.

But Mary was right. If this spell worked, not only would I be safer, but the Crown would be, too.

"Let's do it." I pretended I didn't see Ethan's jaw clench. Instead, I remained focused on Mary. "I'm guessing you know where we can find a chosen champion of Mars?"

"The Otherworld, of course."

I sighed at the thought of another visit to the Otherworld. The fae might be our allies, but there was something unnerving about being in their presence.

Like I had to be on constant alert for trickery.

Which made sense, since with the fae, one *always* had to be on constant alert for trickery.

"When do we leave?" If we were going, I wanted to get it over with.

"When did you last sleep?"

"Does being knocked unconscious count?"

"It's not the same," she said. "Plus, for you, that was… a while ago."

How long ago *was* it? Time no longer moved for me the same way it used to. The hours that had passed since I'd arrived in the Haven were much longer for me, since I'd been time traveling and spending time in the places I'd visited.

Plus, Mary had a good point. I was tired. And in the Otherworld, I needed to be on full alert.

"Let's rest for the night," I said. "We'll go to the Otherworld tomorrow."

"A wise choice." She looked at me approvingly, as if she were seeing me as a Queen instead of someone who'd been newly thrown into the supernatural world.

But even if she saw me as a Queen, I definitely didn't feel like one.

"I'll stay in your room," Ethan said to me. "To keep you safe."

"No," I said, and he winced, as if I'd physically hurt him. "I'm staying with my mom."

The thought of being alone filled me with dread. It wouldn't be the same without knowing Mira was safe in the room next to mine. And I couldn't stay with Ethan. What could I possibly say to him right now? I had too many emotions coursing through me to keep them straight.

What he'd done made no sense. Why hadn't he been honest about his feelings from the start? If he had, none of this would have happened. Mira wouldn't have gone dark.

My twin sister wouldn't *hate* me.

I felt a pang of emptiness surge through me at the reminder of everything I'd lost.

Thanks to the nightshade, I'd had a taste of what it was like to have Ethan love me, but it wasn't real. Now, I didn't have Mira, either.

The never-ending abyss of dark, painful emotions was too much to process. Especially when I had a mission to focus on.

A mission I refused to fail.

Mom rushed to my side, like she was protecting me. "You'll stay in my room," she said, and I nodded, blinking back tears.

We walked back in silence, and the moment I got in bed, I instantly fell asleep.

10

GEMMA

Ethan, Genevieve, and I met with Mary in the tearoom the next morning. I'd had breakfast in the room with Mom, and she'd remained positive, assuring me that we'd get Mira back safely, and all would be well. I'd bring Mira back from the darkness, like I'd done for Torrence. I did it once, so there was no reason I couldn't do it again.

I wasn't sure if she'd been trying to convince me, or herself.

Thanks to Earth's alliance with the Otherworld, Mary had portal tokens that led directly into Sorcha's courtyard. She handed them to us and opened the secret door in the tearoom that led to the small room with the fountain that connected our world to theirs.

The token had a depiction of Sorcha's eerily perfect

face on one side, and her tall crown on the other. Her crown was larger and more embellished than mine, but it was all for show.

Mine was the one with true power.

I reached for it to touch the crystals, and they warmed, like they were alive.

Alive with *magic*.

We all held our tokens and faced the fountain.

Genevieve shifted uneasily on her feet.

"Are you nervous?" I asked, stunned that someone who exuded such confidence could be nervous about *anything*.

"I've never visited the Otherworld before," she said. "And the fae... they're dangerous."

"They're our allies."

"They have the same goal as us, so they're playing nice," she said. "I don't support the dark witches, but there's a reason they put that curse on the fae to banish them to the Otherworld."

The curse that made them allergic to iron—which made it nearly impossible for them to live on Earth.

"They'll help us," I said. "Just like they helped us get to Ember."

"You mean how they let you walk into their *prison world*?"

She had a good point, since it hadn't cost the fae

anything to let us walk into Ember. But I wasn't going to admit it.

"You said you'd help us," I said. "So, are you going to come with us or not?"

"I said I'd work with a chosen champion of Mars to cast the spell on you," she said. "However, I don't see why I have to accompany you to the Otherworld, when you can simply bring a chosen champion of Mars here."

This was taking too long. I wanted to be in the Otherworld speaking with Sorcha already. "Fine—I'll ask her if she'll allow a chosen champion of Mars to come here," I said. "Happy?"

"Yes." Genevieve backed away from the fountain and returned her portal token to Mary.

"Wait," Ethan said. "We should take the token with us. We'll need it to give to the chosen champion of Mars."

"The Empress has her own portal tokens to get here," Mary said. "But you're right. She might try to bargain with it. She might already try to bargain regarding the chosen champion of Mars."

I cursed, since I hadn't thought of that. And bargaining with fae was serious business. They were tricky with their words.

But I was a reader *and* a writer. Well, sort of a writer,

if journaling counted. The point was, I was good with words.

I could do this. Plus, I had Ethan's help. We'd figure it out.

I took the extra token from Mary and put it in my pocket. I was back to wearing my Haven whites, and while they were comfortable, I *did* miss my regular clothes from home.

"I'll be careful," I promised.

"You're a Queen," she said. "Your status is equal to the Empress. Remember that."

"I will."

With that, I stepped back over to Ethan's side, purposefully looking into the fountain instead of at him.

I tossed my token into the water.

Ethan did the same.

The water swirled sparkly purple. He took my hand, and together, we jumped through the portal.

11

GEMMA

W<small>E LANDED</small> on the marble floor of Sorcha's courtyard, I let go of Ethan's hand and tumbled right into someone.

A fae with orange wings.

But the fae barely paid me any attention. Because *tons* of fae were gathered in the courtyard. So many of them that they filled the entire space. I stood up, taking in the scene.

The ones in the center cowered together, holding hands with fear in their eyes.

The ones on the outside—mostly ones with steel gray wings—held weapons at the ready, preparing for a fight.

Thumps sounded against the walls around us. One after the other, never stopping.

Then, there were the groans. Deep, inhuman, *hungry*

groans. Chills ran up and down my spine at the sound of them.

I'd watched enough episodes of *The Walking Dead* to know that sound anywhere.

Zombies.

They were surrounding the palace. From the sound of it, it wouldn't be long before they broke through.

It was also brighter than it had been the last time I'd been there. A glance up showed me that the protection dome that had been around the city was gone.

The dome must have been obliterated, and then the zombies had piled in.

I searched for Sorcha. Thanks to her white ballgown, it wasn't hard to find her at the center of the courtyard. She stood with her advisor Aeliana, their hands clutched together so tightly that it was like they were holding onto each other for their lives.

I pushed through the crowd to make my way to her. The fae looked at me curiously, but let me pass at the sight of the Crown on my head.

"Sorcha!" I called her name, louder and louder until she heard me.

She spun around, her eyes narrowed in offense—probably at the fact that I hadn't used her royal title to address her. Leave it to Sorcha to care about formalities in a time like this. Then her gaze met mine, and she breathed out in relief.

The crowd parted as she and Aeliana made their way toward me and Ethan.

"You found the Holy Crown," she said simply.

"What happened here?" I didn't bother answering her question, since yes, obviously I'd found the Crown.

"The boundary dome around the city was created by Selena," she said. "Since she died, it's been deteriorating. It fully gave way yesterday. We've been doing our best to keep the infected at bay, but..." She looked around helplessly. "There are too many of them for us to stop them."

Aeliana looked at me, her gaze steady and calm. "You haven't come to save us."

"I'm sorry," I said. "I don't have that kind of power. I'm not the Queen of Wands. Or the Queen of Swords."

"Not even the Queen of Swords could fight off this many of them," Sorcha said. "They're everywhere—hordes of them. They can only be killed with holy weapons. And since we can't use holy weapons, we're helpless against them."

"The fae can't use holy weapons because of the iron," Ethan said. "But half-bloods aren't allergic to iron. They can use the weapons."

"Half-bloods have no magic or supernatural strength. Only chosen champions are strong enough to kill the infected," Sorcha said. "But there aren't enough chosen champions to hold off all the infected in the realm. If the half-bloods were free, we'd have a large enough army to slaughter the infected in days. But with their magic bound, the half-bloods are useless."

She said the final part in distaste, as if it were the half-bloods' fault that the fae bound their magic at birth to force them into lives of servitude.

"Selena was going to free them," she continued. "If she hadn't gone off on that quest on Earth that got her killed, she'd have already done it, and we wouldn't be in this position now."

Of course.

That was our answer.

"What would you say if I told you I can save Selena?" I asked.

Sorcha lifted an eyebrow. "You can raise the dead?"

"No. But I can change the past."

"I'm listening."

"The Holy Crown's magic allows me to travel back in time," I said, and I quickly summarized what I'd learned so far about my time traveling abilities. I had to raise my voice to be heard over the chaos, but I managed to relay all of it to Sorcha.

I didn't tell her about Mira going dark. We didn't have time for that.

Well, technically, the Crown could give me time for anything. But Sorcha was desperate right now. Which was where I wanted her, so whatever bargain she was sure to propose would be in my favor.

"I can't walk around in the past with the Holy Crown on my head," I explained. "It would bring unwanted attention and potentially make me a target. But if I take it off, I risk it being stolen. I need a safe place to keep it while I'm traveling."

The thumps against the palace walls were getting louder.

Sorcha looked around, worried. "What do you think I can do for you?"

"I need you to command a chosen champion of Mars to come to the Haven with me." I knew from my studies that the fae with steel gray wings who were guarding the outskirts of the courtyard were chosen champions of Mars. "The most powerful witch on Earth has promised to try using the chosen champion's magic to cast a spell on me and the Crown so I can store it in the ether. I have an extra portal token for them to use."

"And in return?" Sorcha asked.

"I'll do everything in my power to save Selena."

"Deal."

No way, I thought, shocked. That was far easier than

it should have been. Although maybe not, given Sorcha's current predicament.

I was tempted to thank her, but I held back.

Never thank a fae. Doing so binds you to a favor of their choice.

"You won't regret this," I said instead.

"I know." She turned to the nearest steel winged guard. "Gaius!" she called out, and he hurried toward us and bowed his head to Sorcha.

"Your Highness." He was big and rough around the edges, but soft spoken.

"I need you to accompany the Queen of Pentacles to the Haven," she said. "She'll explain your purpose there after you arrive. You can trust her."

An ear-splitting crack erupted from the other side of the courtyard.

The door had broken open.

Milky-eyed, black-winged, rotted fae-zombies dragged themselves through the opening.

Steel winged fae rushed forward and stabbed the zombies' hearts with their holy weapons. The zombies turned to ash, leaving piles of it where they'd been standing.

Another crack—this time from the side.

More zombies piled through.

My breathing quickened. I had a holy weapon on me,

but I wasn't skilled enough to fight so many of them at once. Besides, once I saved Selena, whether or not I stayed to help should be irrelevant.

"Do you have a portal token?" I asked the Empress.

She shook her head no.

But Aeliana had future sight. Surely, she'd known to prepare.

"And you?" I asked her.

"We do not," Aeliana said calmly.

The Empress straightened. "I'll be by the sides of my people until the very end."

Ethan nodded in respect. "A noble choice."

"Now, go." Sorcha motioned toward the fountain. "You can't save Selena if you become food for the infected."

"When we return, this will never have happened," I told her. "The Otherworld will be safe. You won't remember any of this."

"But you'll tell me, so I'll know?"

"I will."

Maybe.

The zombies moved in closer. One of them reached a pink winged fae who'd been pushed to the side, pulled her in, and took a giant bite out of her forearm.

Her scream sliced the air, and my nerves buzzed with warning.

Time to bolt.

I handed the extra portal token to Gaius. He cleared the way toward the fountain for me and Ethan, and then the three of us tossed our tokens into the water and jumped in, leaving the terrified screams, hungry groans, and foul scent of death behind us.

12

GEMMA

THE SILENCE when we landed back in the Haven was a sharp contrast to the palace's chaos.

Mary and Genevieve were sitting on the benches in the tearoom, drinking and eating snacks, as if everything were perfectly normal.

Genevieve startled at our arrival. "That was fast," she said, although she wasn't looking at us—she was looking at Gaius.

His wings had gone invisible, since he was on Earth. He eyed her suspiciously, and his huge muscles flexed, clearly on guard.

It made sense, given the strained relationship between the fae and the witches.

Regardless, Genevieve placed her teacup down and

smiled seductively. "I see why the god of war blessed you with his magic."

He barely acknowledged her before turning to me. "Tell me why I'm here."

Mary stood, and all attention went to her. "I'm Mary, the ruler of the Haven—one of Earth's seven supernatural kingdoms," she introduced herself. "Please sit and help yourself to whatever you'd like to eat."

"Tell me why I'm here," he repeated.

Apparently, he was a man of few words.

Genevieve huffed in irritation. "It's tradition to break bread before discussing political matters," she said. "By not doing so, you're offending the queen."

Mary didn't like to be called a queen—even though she was, technically, a queen—but she didn't bother to correct the witch.

He glanced at me. "I thought you were the queen."

"I'm a different type of queen," I said, and his brow furrowed in confusion. "Break bread with us, and we'll explain everything."

"The food is safe?"

"I promise."

He hesitated, then said, "The Empress said to trust you. So, I'll trust you."

I stopped myself from pointing out that he didn't

have much of a choice, since his realm was destroyed and his only chance of getting it back was to trust me.

He'd learn that soon.

"Thank you." I purposefully used the words that were avoided in the Otherworld. The words only bound a person to a favor for full fae—not half-bloods—but by using them, I hoped to show vulnerability.

He made a soft sound of approval, then sat as far away from Genevieve as possible.

She bristled and refused to meet his eyes.

Mary prepared him a plate and handed it to him. He hesitated, then took a bite of buttery naan. It was a good choice, since the Indian flatbread was a specialty in the Haven. As he chewed, his eyes lit up, and he inhaled the rest of it in a few bites.

Mary smiled and placed a full plate of naan in front of him. She also poured him a cup of spicy tea.

He picked up the cup and took a small sip. His lips pursed in distaste, and he placed it back down and took another large bite of naan.

"What type of drink is that?" he asked after swallowing.

"Masala chai," she said.

He took another sip, not looking as startled this time. "Drinks in the Otherworld are all sweet," he said. "Apologies if I offended you."

"No worries," she said. "I understand that this realm is foreign to you. But, now that we've broken bread, we must tell you why you're here."

"We're here to save the Otherworld," he said simply, and Genevieve's eyebrow raised in surprise. "The Empress thought I would be more useful here than there."

"*Save* the Otherworld?" Genevieve repeated, and she looked to me and Ethan for answers.

"We went through the portal and arrived to total chaos," I said, and from there, I told them everything that had happened from the moment we'd entered the Otherworld until now.

After they'd been filled in, we told Gaius our predicament.

"We need to create a space in the ether for me to store the Holy Crown," I said. "Will you help us?"

"The Queen of Wands must be saved," he said. "Of course I'll help you."

"Good," said Genevieve. "Are you both ready to get this over with?"

"Yes," I said, at the same time as Gaius.

"All right," she said. "Obviously I've never done a

spell of this nature before. So, I'm just going to go with my intuition."

"Sounds good to me." I'd always trusted my intuition, and since Genevieve was a powerful witch, I assumed she had good intuition, too.

Ethan turned to me, worried. "Are you sure about this?"

"Of course I'm sure." I brushed off his concern, focusing on Genevieve instead. "What do you need me to do?"

"Keep the Crown on," she said, and I nodded, since I hadn't intended to take it off. "I'm going to take both of your hands and try to channel Gaius's magic into you."

"Sounds good."

She stood between me and Gaius and took both of our hands. Then she closed her eyes and started chanting in Latin.

I closed my eyes, too. I didn't like seeing the others staring at me.

Mainly. I didn't like seeing *Ethan* staring at me. It was too tempting to stare back.

As Genevieve chanted, warm magic rushed into my palm and traveled up to the Crown. The Crown tingled with an explosion of light, the crystals buzzing like they were creating magical strands to connect with the Universe.

Genevieve stopped chanting, and the magic receded. She pulled her hand out of mine, and I opened my eyes.

Mary watched us expectantly. "Did it work?"

Genevieve gave her a knowing smile, then turned to me. "Let's have Gemma show us."

"Okay." I reached for the Crown, removed it from my head, and looked to Gaius. This was going to work. It *had* to work. "What do I do?"

"Imagine a cubby next to your shoulder," he said. "Picture it and feel it. Then, reach for it and place the Crown inside."

"You make it sound so easy."

"It is. Give it a go."

I did exactly as Gaius said, and as I held the Crown over my shoulder, I felt the air *opening*. The Crown slid inside an invisible "cubby" and disappeared. Half of my hand was in there, too.

"You can let go of it," Gaius said.

I held my breath. This would be the first time I'd let the Crown out of my sight since Ethan had placed it on my head in Antarctica. I'd even been keeping it on while sleeping.

I breathed out at the same time as I let go of the Crown, and worry tugged at my lungs.

"Good," Gaius said. "Now, reach back into the ether and take it back."

Not wasting a second, I did as he'd instructed. The ether parted as easily for me as it had the first time, and the moment my hand was inside, I felt the Crown's crystals on my fingertips.

I pulled it out and placed it on my head.

Where it belonged.

Every muscle in my body relaxed once it was in place.

I tested the "ether cubby," a few more times, and didn't have any issues with it.

"Glad we got that figured out," I said once I was positive I'd gotten the hang of it, keeping my focus on Mary. "Now... do you have any ideas about how to save Selena?"

"Not quite," she said. "But I know someone who will."

"Who?"

"The people who saw her last. Reed and Torrence."

"Good plan," I said, since at least it was something to start with.

"I'll send a fire message to tell them to come here tomorrow," she said.

"Why tomorrow?"

"Because before we get any more people involved, there are a few more things we need to learn about how your magic works."

13

GEMMA

TORRENCE AND REED arrived in the Haven the next day, where they met with me, Ethan, and Mary in the tearoom.

Torrence's eyes bulged when she saw the Holy Crown on my head. "I guess you found the other half of it."

"Had to go all the way to Antarctica, but yes, we got the second half of the Crown," I said.

"Antarctica," she repeated. "Sounds like quite the adventure."

"You have no idea."

She looked around, like she was searching for someone else, then refocused on me. "Where's Mira?"

My heart broke all over again at the sound of my sister's name.

Torrence frowned. "I guess she wasn't happy that you're the Queen of Pentacles and not her."

Understatement of the century.

"We should sit down," I said. "Because we have a lot to catch you up on."

Torrence and Reed listened attentively as we told them everything that had happened since parting ways in Ember.

"I have an idea about how to save Selena," I said, and I turned to Reed. "But I'll need your help."

"I'm listening."

"You, Selena, Julian, and the Supreme Mages worked together to find Torrence on Circe's island," I started, and he nodded for me to continue. "I can travel back to when the group of you were together and talk to Selena. I'll tell her what happens, so she's prepared."

"You'll tell her that the Supreme Mages are going to turn on her, killing her and her soulmate?" he said, continuing before I could answer. "Because I don't think that will go over well. Besides, we spent the entire time searching for Torrence on a ship. It was the best way to make sure no witches, mages, or demons interrupted our trip."

"Because they can't teleport onto a ship if they haven't been on that ship, and even so, they can't get there if the ship's moving," I said, remembering what I'd learned while on board the Golden Moon for the Antarctica cruise.

"Exactly."

"You were on a ship the entire time?" Ethan asked.

"We were," Reed said. "As the Queen of Wands, Selena was a target. We didn't want any demons popping in uninvited and attacking."

It was smart.

Unfortunately, it made things harder for us.

Way harder.

"When did you first get on the ship?" My stomach knotted as I waited for the answer.

"Right after Christmas."

I cursed at his answer.

"What's wrong?" Torrence asked.

"I can't travel back to before I received my elemental magic." I'd learned that during the tests I'd conducted with Mary, but hadn't thought it would be an issue, seeing as Selena had been killed *months* after I'd gotten my magic.

"What?" Torrence balked. "Why not?"

"I don't know."

"Well... is there a way you can find out?"

I almost said no, but I stopped myself.

Because there *was* a way I could find out.

"Maybe," I said, standing up. "Can you wait here for a moment?"

Confusion crossed over her features. "Where are you going?"

"To a place where I might be able to get an answer." Without bothering to explain—since there'd be no *point*—I walked over to the door, used my key, and stepped into the ivory hall of the Eternal Library.

I smiled at the sight of Hecate standing there, waiting for me.

Why was she there sometimes, and not others?

I shelved that as a question to ask her in the future. Because right now, we had bigger issues to deal with.

I'd only taken a few steps toward her when the door opened, and Ethan stepped through.

Irritation ran through me. "I know it's your duty to protect me and all, but I'm safe in the Eternal Library," I said.

"I know you're safe here. I also see that Hecate's here." He nodded to her in greeting, and she returned the gesture. "It's better that we're able to ask two questions instead of only one."

I frowned, since his point was a good one, then spun back around to face Hecate. "It's good to see you," I said.

"You, too," she said with a knowing smile. "I assume you're prepared with a question?"

"I am."

"Then follow me, and I'll get your answers."

We walked with her into the hall of bookshelves. It looked the exact same as always, as if the never-ending shelves were trapped in time.

She took her spot in front of the podium, focused on me, and waited.

"My time travel magic is limited—it doesn't let me travel back to before I received my elemental magic." I phrased the start of what I was getting at as a statement, so it wouldn't be confused for my actual question. "How can I travel back to before that moment as easily and consistently as I can travel back to the times after it?"

Hecate turned to the shelves, and the cosmic mist poured out of her eyes and traveled down the hall. It didn't take long before a book soared toward us and into her hands. The book was a soft cream color, and warm, welcoming magic pulsed out of it.

The cosmic mist returned to Hecate's body, the breeze from it flipping through the book's pages until landing on one about three quarters of the way through.

Hecate pressed her lips together in concentration as she read. Once done, she pulled the book closer and looked to us. "The Crown was weakened when it was broken in half," she said. "It's magic won't be at full capacity until it's mended. *You're* able to mend it, but you can't do that until you become stronger. To become strong enough to mend the Crown, you must eat the food of the Heavens—mana."

There was only one place I knew of where mana could be found.

"Looks like we're going to Avalon," I said, and Hecate nodded, as if letting me know it was the right decision.

"Ethan?" she asked.

I didn't look at him. I couldn't. I just... couldn't. It hurt too badly.

"What's the name of the person who enspelled the cuffs that are keeping the dragons on Ember enslaved?" he asked.

Really? He'd asked about the dragons on Ember instead of something that would help us save Mira *again*?

Freeing the dragons can help us save Mira, I reminded myself. *They're our allies. They'll fight with us.*

It still didn't stop me from resenting the fact that he wasn't taking a more direct approach.

Hecate brought forth another book with her cosmic mist. This one was dark gray.

She barely had to glance at the open page to get the answer. "Supreme Mage Ragnarr Bell," she said, and I couldn't help it—I glanced at Ethan to see his reaction.

He froze, shellshocked, like he didn't know what to think. "The King of the Dark Mages," he finally said, although he spoke slowly, like the words were strange and foreign.

"Yes," Hecate said.

"But Supreme Mages can't be killed."

Hecate said nothing.

Yet another question for another day.

"Thank you for all your help," I told her. "Hopefully we'll see you soon."

"Perhaps." She smiled knowingly, then the books flew back to their shelves, and she disappeared.

I spun around angrily to face Ethan. "You *knew* one of the dark mages on Ember enspelled those cuffs," I said. "Why did you waste a question on that?"

"I didn't know exactly which mage it was," he said. "The fact that it's the King of the Dark Mages—a *Supreme Mage*—is huge. We needed that information."

"We *need* more help to save Mira."

"You're angry at me."

"You think?" There was no containing the sarcasm that dripped from my tone.

"Gemma." He reached for me, but I stepped away, and sadness crossed over his features. "Talk to me."

"How am I supposed to talk to you when I can't *trust* you?"

The moment it came out of my mouth, I understood the core of the emotion I'd buried deep inside me.

Distrust.

Ethan had lied to me. He'd lied to Mira. His lies had destroyed all three of us.

How was I supposed to be able to trust him after all we'd been through?

"You can trust me," he said. "I'm here for you, always."

"You're here to protect me physically," I said. "But emotionally? You've…" I paused, searching for the right word.

Hurt me?

That was the understatement of the century.

Betrayed me?

Getting closer.

Destroyed me.

Yes. That was what I felt like inside right now. *Destroyed*. Ripped into so many shreds that I didn't think I'd ever be able to be put back together again.

"I can't do this right now," I said instead, and I hurried out into the ivory hall and toward the door.

I didn't glance over my shoulder to see if Ethan was behind me.

Because if there was one thing I *did* trust, it was that he'd always chase me when I ran.

14

GEMMA

Torrence, Reed, and Mary were eating sugary pastries in the tearoom when we returned.

Mary stared at me and set her teacup down. "She was there."

Apparently, she was able to tell that I'd spoken to Hecate simply from my expression.

"She was," I said.

"Who was where?" Torrence asked.

"The goddess of witches, Hecate," I said, completely deadpan. "She was waiting for us in her Eternal Library, where she used her cosmic magic to find books with the answers to our questions."

Torrence's eyes went blank, then refocused. "I've heard the Haven library is extensive," she said. "Not *nearly* as extensive as the Devereux library, but I'm glad their librarian was able to get our answer."

"What's the answer?" Reed asked, as if Torrence hadn't totally misheard what I'd said.

"The Crown was weakened when it was broken in half," I said. "To fix it, I need to strengthen my magic."

"How do you do that?"

"I need to eat mana."

"Mana can't leave Avalon," Reed said. "It decomposes the moment anyone tries to bring it off the island."

"I know." That was one of the many things I'd learned in my time in Utopia. "We can't bring the mana to me. Which means I need to go to the mana."

"You're coming to Avalon?" Torrence's eyes lit up.

"I'm going to *try* to go to Avalon," I said. "I still haven't gone through the Angel Trials."

"You'll pass," she said, like there was no question about it.

"I thought Harper would pass, too," I said. "We *all* thought she'd pass."

"That's different. I mean, yes, it was surprising Harper didn't pass, given how strong her magic is. But you're one of the Four Holy Queens. Avalon is meant to be your home."

Home.

The thought of finally getting what I'd been missing ever since receiving my magic should have warmed me.

Instead, I felt nothing.

"Home is where my mom and sister are," I said instead.

Ever since leaving Australia, it had been true. I just hadn't realized it until now.

And it's where Ethan is, that annoying little voice in the back of my head reminded me.

"Your mom will enter the Angel Trials, too," Ethan said. "And then, once Mira's back, so will she."

"And then what?" I said bitterly. "The four of us will live happily ever after?"

"We'll be safe," he said, and he turned to Mary. "Bring Rachael here. Also send for three witches, because me, Gemma, and Rachael will immediately go to the Vale so we can enter the Angel Trials."

"One witch," Torrence corrected him. "Reed and I can take two of you. We'll drop you off at the Vale, and then, we'll see you in Avalon."

15

GEMMA

THE CANADIAN ROCKIES were the biggest mountains I'd ever seen, towering high into the starry night sky. The Vale's palace and surrounding towns were built into it, like they'd been born out of the rocks. The palace was near the peak, and the rest of the buildings sprawled out below. Lights glowed from inside of them, the only warmth in the cold night.

I inhaled the crisp, thin air and gazed out at the fresh, powdery snow that covered the mountains. It was beautiful—more like something you'd see on a postcard than in real life.

We'd arrived outside the boundary dome, where Harper and two other witches were waiting for us.

Harper's eyes met mine, and she beamed. Her long, dark hair was shinier than ever, and while she was paler than before, her skin was positively radiant. Also, she was wearing jeans, a black tank, and a leather jacket. I'd never seen her in everyday clothes, and she looked stunning. If she'd walked down the halls of my school, she would have turned every guys' head.

She teleported next to me and threw her arms around me in a hug.

She smelled like a mix of flowers and metal. Witch and vampire. A strange combination, but then again, hers was a strange situation.

She pulled back and studied me—well, she studied the Holy Crown. "The Queen of Pentacles," she said with a smile. "Who would have thought?"

"Definitely not you." I laughed, remembering how frustrated Harper had been during our lessons. I'd had the hardest time getting the hang of my magic.

"Not true." She stuck her tongue out at me. "I always knew you had potential. Especially after you blasted through the rocks to create that escape cave..." She trailed off and looked out to the mountains, her eyes sad.

Because I'd created the cave that allowed us to escape Utopia.

It was the day Harper's kingdom had been destroyed and her mother killed.

"This is where we leave you," Torrence said, and she

gave me a knowing look. One that said, *you better pass the Trials, because we need to save Selena.* "We'll see the three of you in Avalon."

"See you there," I said, and then she and Reed teleported out.

My mom wrapped her arms around herself, shifting from one foot to the other on the snow-covered ground. "Any chance we can get inside?" she asked. "All of you might be immune to the cold, but I'm about to turn into an ice cube."

"Of course," Harper said. "King Alexander and Queen Deidre are waiting in the throne room. We'll bring you straight there."

She took my hands, the other two witches took Mom's and Ethan's, and the group of us teleported inside the Vale.

One moment we were in the cold mountains, and the next, we were in the palace, facing a man and a woman sitting on matching ornate thrones. They each wore golden crowns and were dressed like they were attending a black-tie affair. But judging from the more casual outfits worn by the guards and the witches, their attire wasn't the norm in the Vale.

They both stood, which caught me off guard. Because royalty didn't stand for anyone except…

"Queen Gemma," the man—King Alexander—greeted me. "Welcome to the Vale."

Royalty didn't stand for anyone except other royalty.

"King Alexander." I bowed my head slightly. "Queen Deidre."

"It's nice to meet you," Deidre said.

"And you," I replied. "This is my mom. And this…" I paused, unsure how to describe my relationship with Ethan.

My protector?

My sister's ex?

My twin flame?

"Ethan Pendragon." He stepped forward and introduced himself. "The King of Ember."

"The dragon realm," said a man standing to King Alexander's side. "Fascinating. I'm Rohan, by the way. *Prince* Rohan. Harper's boyfriend."

Harper's *boyfriend?*

I looked to her in surprise, and she smiled sheepishly.

No. Way.

Rohan was a vampire.

The supernatural women of Utopia wanted nothing to do with supernatural men.

Rohan must be *really* special to have broken down Harper's walls.

King Alexander cleared his throat, as if he were telling Rohan to mind his place. "Harper has told us much about you and your sister," he said. "But only up to the last time she saw you, when you slayed the vampire who was tracking your dragon magic."

"I know you've come here to enter the Angel Trials," Queen Deidre continued. "However, we were hoping you might stay for dinner. The demons and dark witches pose a major threat to the supernatural kingdoms, and it's important that we share as much as we can with our allies so we can all stay safe."

They wanted information.

After what had happened to Utopia, I didn't blame them. Besides, we'd need as much support as possible when it came to freeing the dragons. The more people we could get on our side, the better.

"We'd love to stay for dinner," Ethan said, apparently having the same idea.

"Wonderful." Deidre beamed. "Dinner isn't for another three hours. Perhaps you'd like a tour of the kingdom beforehand?"

"That would be lovely," I said. "But I'd like to spend some time with Harper first. As you noted, we haven't seen each other in a while. And we have a *lot* to catch each other up on."

I glanced at Rohan at that last part.

Harper's cheeks turned pink.

I never thought I'd see the day when Harper actually *blushed*.

"Of course," Deidre said. "I'll personally see to the start of your mom and King Ethan's tour. You and Harper can join us after you've convened."

"Great." Harper was by my side in a second. "I'll take you to my room."

"We'll see you girls soon," Deidre said, and then Harper grabbed my hands, and teleported us out.

16

GEMMA

"Where's Mira?" Harper asked the moment we landed in her room.

Every organ in my body collapsed at the mention of my twin's name.

"I don't know," I said helplessly, gazing around her room. It was plush, with a king-sized bed with a silk comforter on it, a sitting area for meals, and a balcony that overlooked the town.

It was the total opposite of anything in Utopia.

"What do you mean, you don't know?" she asked.

"I mean that I don't know." I sighed and sat on Harper's bed. "A lot's happened since we last saw each other."

"I can see that." She joined me on the bed, plucked a pillow from the giant pile of them against the headboard, and held it on her lap with her arms wrapped around it. "Want to start from the beginning?"

"Only if you tell me what's been going on with you, too."

"Deal," she said, and from there, we filled each other in on everything that had happened since we'd last seen each other in Lilith's lair.

"Wow," Harper said once we were both caught up on each other's lives. "That's... a lot."

"Tell me about it."

"What do you know about the Dark Objects?" she asked.

"Honestly? Not much." I frowned, since questions about the Dark Objects needed to be added to the list of things to ask Hecate.

"Then it's a good thing I've been looking into them," she said. "Well, that *Rohan* and I have been looking into them. He's been more helpful than I'd thought he'd be."

"Why have you been looking into the Dark Objects?" I asked.

"I'll tell you in a moment," she said. "But first, you need to know that just because someone is the Queen—or King—of a Dark Object, it doesn't mean they're evil."

"There are Kings of the Objects?"

"Rarely. And usually, they don't last for long. Azazel was the Dark King of Cups before Raven killed him."

"Who got the Dark Grail after him?" I asked.

"Lilith."

I sighed, since of *course* the Demon Queen was also one of the Dark Queens. Why should I have expected anything less?

"The point is that just because Mira has the Dark Crown, it doesn't mean she's gone totally dark," Harper continued. "We can still save her."

"How do you know all of this?"

"How else?" She reached for the key hanging from her necklace. "I asked Hecate."

Relief flooded my veins, since Hecate wouldn't lie.

At least, I thought she wouldn't. My gut told me to trust that what she told us from the books was what she'd actually read in them.

"We know that Lavinia took Mira," I said. "And that Lavinia's working with Lilith. The three of them have to be together."

"It would make sense," Harper agreed.

"Have you gotten any closer to figuring out the location of Lilith's lair?"

"No," she said. "I asked Hecate, but even she doesn't

know. Whatever magic is hiding the lair is too strong for her to break through."

"So how are we supposed to find them?"

"By using the same technique we did in Nebraska," she said. "By getting them to come to us."

"And how do you propose we do that?"

"By finding something they need. In this case, the fourth Dark Object. The Dark Sword."

"You have it?" I looked around the room, as if she might be hiding it in a drawer or in her closet.

"Rohan and I are working on it," she said. "We were thinking we'd find it to weaken Lilith. Because if we find the Dark Sword and hide it somewhere she can't find it—someplace like Avalon—then she won't be able to get her fourth Dark Queen."

"But we can also use it to draw out Lilith."

"We can," she said, and she paused, like she didn't think I was going to like what she had to say next. "Although I think we should wait until after you've saved Selena, and after we have the dragons fighting on our side. Not like it matters what I think, since we have three—soon to be four—Holy Queens, seven vampire kingdoms, and multiple realms working together. Everyone will have a say on how to find and defeat Lilith, Lavinia, and the demons and dark witches."

"True," I said, since together, there was no reason why we shouldn't be able to defeat the demons. "But how can you know that Lilith doesn't have the Dark Sword?"

"Lavinia told me when I was transitioning into a vampire," she said. "She thought I was trapped there, so she was pretty open with information."

"So you didn't get your gift until after you completed your transition?"

"That's right."

"I'm really happy for you," I said. "I can't imagine you without your witch magic."

"Neither could I," she said. "I'd like to think I would have come to terms with it... but I don't know. I was devastated during those days in the transition when my magic was gone."

"Now you're a witch, *and* you're immortal."

"Stuck as a teenager forever." She made a face. "Just what I always wanted." Sarcasm dripped from her tone.

"It won't be that bad," I said, even though I wouldn't have wanted to be stuck as a teen forever, either. "Luckily, you don't look too young. With the right clothes and makeup, you can easily pass for in your twenties."

"That's what I keep telling myself." She pulled the pillow closer to her chest and looked around the room.

"Are you happy here?" I asked.

"Sure." She smiled, although it wasn't convincing.

"Rohan's great. The other witches are warming up to me a bit, although I think it might be because Queen Deidre told them to be more welcoming. It's just…"

"You wish you were in Avalon?"

"Surprisingly, no," she said. "But I do wish I knew why I didn't pass the Angel Trials."

"You really don't remember any of it?"

"None. One moment I was walking through the portal that led to the start of the Trials, and the next I was floating in the rowboat that brought me back to the Vale."

"To the riverbank where Rohan was waiting for you." I gave her a small smile, hoping to lift her spirits at the reminder of the man she was in love with—even if she hadn't put it in those exact words.

"Yeah."

"Do you think you're here because *he's* here?"

"Of course you'd think that," she said, finally smiling again. "You've always been a hopeless romantic. Speaking of…"

"I don't want to talk about him," I said abruptly.

"Okay." She frowned, then continued, "Maybe part of the reason why I'm here is because of Rohan. He's definitely why I wouldn't want to go to Avalon anymore. But I also think I'm supposed to be working with him to research the Dark Sword. I can't explain why… but trying to find information about it *feels* right."

"Witch intuition?" I guessed.

"Maybe. Or maybe I want to feel like I have a purpose."

"You have a purpose," I said, feeling the truth of it deep in my soul. "Everyone does. Besides, I don't think a purpose is something we *have* as much as something we find inside ourselves. And if it feels right to search for the Dark Sword, then I believe you're meant to be searching for the Dark Sword."

"I just wish we could find some kind of lead," she said. "We've traced it up until the early 1900s. After that, it's like it disappeared off the face of the planet."

"Maybe that's it," I said.

"Maybe *what's* it?"

"Lilith has the dragon heart, which is how she tracked down the Dark Wand and the Dark Crown," I started. "But dragon hearts can't track outside the realm they're in."

"So the Dark Sword isn't on Earth?"

"Seems like a strong possibility. Either that, or she already has it, or someone else already has it and is protecting it with a spell that even the dragon heart can't get past."

"All good theories," she said. "I'll look into them."

"Where are you looking?"

"The Vale's library," she said. "And Hecate's. Although Rohan obviously doesn't know about Hecate's. He just thinks I'm *really* good at looking through books." She chuckled, and I did, too, since Harper had always referred to the history books we had to read for our studies in Utopia as the "boring books."

"Speaking of purposes," she said, serious again. "I have a request."

"Name it."

"I want you to bring us back in time to before Utopia was destroyed. And then I want to find Queen Elizabeth and warn her about what's going to happen, so she can make whatever preparations she needs to save my kingdom and everyone in it."

17

GEMMA

"I don't know if I can," I said, and she slumped forward slightly.

"Why?"

"Because if I do anything in the past that makes it so Mira or I don't get our Crowns—or that *any* of the Queens don't get their objects—time will reject the change. I'll come back and everything will be the same as before I left."

"But you don't *know* that saving Utopia will make it so the two of you don't get the Crowns."

"I don't. But that would be a *huge* change…"

"Can we at least try?" she asked. "For me?" Her eyes were huge and desperate, and I understood why.

If I'd lost everything, I'd do anything to get it back, too.

"Of course we can try," I said. "I just don't want you to get your hopes up."

"I understand there's a chance it might not work," she said. "But if we don't try, then there's *zero* chance it'll work."

"I know," I said. "We can try."

She smiled, looking truly happy for the first time since I'd arrived at the Vale, and then we created a plan.

It was rushed, and I doubted Time would accept such a huge change. But I was happy to see Harper happy.

"Let's go now," she said. "We have to be back before dinner. Queen Deidre *hates* when people are late."

"I can time travel, remember?" I said. "I can never be late. No matter how much time we spend in Utopia, it'll be like no time passed in the present. We'll return to the second after we left."

"Perfect," she said, and then she reached for her key and hurried to the door. She put her key in the lock and stepped through before I could say another word—like she was afraid I'd try to stop her.

I rushed into the Eternal Library right after her, glad she was still in the ivory hall when I got there.

There was also someone noticeably missing from the ivory hall—Hecate. Although I shouldn't have been surprised, given how rarely the goddess made her appearances. But still, the chance of seeing Hecate was why we always opted to go through the Library with Harper instead of teleporting to our destination.

"Before we go," I said, and I took a deep breath, unsure how to launch into what needed to be said. "Have you been to Utopia since Lavinia's attack?"

"No," she said. "Have you?"

"No. But I think we need to prepare ourselves for what we're going to see."

"The aftermath of a war zone." She straightened, her eyes hard. "I know."

"Okay. Do you want to enter via the apartment I stayed in while there?" It wasn't a question as much as a statement. Because I didn't know what would happen if we walked into Harper's house, but I couldn't imagine that seeing the place where you'd grown up in shambles would be good for anyone.

I also didn't know if there'd be remains of people who'd lived there inside.

I shuddered at the thought.

But the Nephilim and witches had done "reconnaissance" in Utopia. I hoped that meant they'd cleared out the bodies.

"My apartment was always empty during the days, since Mira and I were in our classes and Mom was working in the bakery," I added, since it was important that no one witnessed our sudden appearance.

The less we changed in the past, the better.

"Good plan," she said, and then she walked up to the door, stuck her key in it, and left the Library.

I followed at her heels.

The scene was as expected—a war zone. Tables and chairs were toppled over. The beds had been pushed aside, as if people had been searching under them. Candlesticks and books had been knocked off nightstands. The wardrobe doors were open, clothes thrown out and strewn around the rooms.

Harper looked around, her expression giving away none of her feelings. "What do we do from here?" she asked.

"I'll take your hands," I said. "It's sort of like teleporting, except we'll be traveling into the past."

"Through time," she said, mystified.

"Exactly." I walked toward her and took her hands. The Crown was already on my head, since I'd worn it to the Vale. No need to hide it in the ether when I'd been making a point of displaying my new position as Queen. "You ready?"

"I'm ready."

I closed my eyes and thought about the time we wanted to go to. The Crown warmed, we flickered a few times, and for a split-second, the ground disappeared beneath our feet.

I let go of Harper's hands and watched as she opened her eyes.

The apartment was back in perfect condition. It was empty of people, but the scent of fresh coffee lingered in the air from when the past versions of me, Mira, Ethan, and Mom had been getting ready in the morning.

"Impressive." Harper gazed around like she was in a museum.

I walked over and put on a fresh pot of coffee, since the strong smell was our best chance of hiding the fact that Harper now gave off the scents of witch *and* vampire.

"Where are your notebooks and stuff?" she asked, getting straight to business.

"I'll get it." I entered my bedroom, where a notebook was placed neatly on top of a giant history book. I picked it up, along with the pencil next to it, and brought them back to Harper.

She examined the sharpened pencil, opened the notebook, then got to writing.

Gemma and I are in her apartment. We need you to come meet us here now—it's urgent. Come alone and don't tell anyone we're here. Also, don't reply to this letter. We'll explain everything in person.

She signed it and folded it. Then she glanced at me. "You should probably take that Crown off," she said.

"Right." I'd become so used to the weight of the Crown on my head that I barely noticed it anymore. When I took it off and stored it in the ether, it was like a part of me was missing. But it was safe there. That was what mattered.

Harper placed the letter in her open palm, then engulfed it in flames. The flames died out, and the letter was gone. Not even ash remained. Because it wasn't a real fire—it was witch magic.

"How long do you think she'll be?" I asked.

"No one ever speaks to Queen Elizabeth like that," she said. "I don't imagine it'll be long."

Sure enough, Queen Elizabeth burst through the apartment door minutes later. The shrunken heads on her belt rustled against each other as she slammed the door shut. "You summoned me?" She stood tall, her nearly six-foot frame towering over us. From the edge in her tone, it was clear she was thinking that whatever we had to say better be good. Then, she froze and asked, "What are you wearing?"

"Gemma's wearing Haven whites," Harper said, even though Queen Elizabeth obviously knew what Haven whites looked like. "I'm wearing civilian clothes, as I've come from the Vale."

Elizabeth narrowed her eyes. "You left Utopia?" She sounded more shocked than anything else.

"We did."

Queen Elizabeth sucked in a long breath, as if she were trying to compose herself. "How could you be so careless?" The iciness in her tone got across one message—there *would* be consequences for this transgression. "The demons are tracking Gemma. You were responsible for keeping her here and giving her lessons to teach her how to control her magic."

"I am giving her lessons," Harper said calmly. "Right now."

"By *bringing her out of my kingdom?*"

Tense energy crackled between the two of them.

"Enough." I stepped forward to stand between them. Yes, we were going for shock value. And yes, I didn't believe anything we did here mattered, since Time would likely reject the changes we made. But it was time to get to the point. "Harper is in the meeting room giving us lessons right now," I said.

Elizabeth's expression changed from anger to confusion. "What are you talking about?"

"Go to the meeting room and check," I said. "We'll be there, in our clothes from Utopia, right now."

She eyed us. "I have guards outside the door," she said, which we knew would be the case. "If you try to leave, they'll attack."

"Understood," I said. "We're not going to leave."

She gave us one final wary look, then left the apartment.

"That went well," Harper said after the door was closed.

"You were goading her."

"I was getting her attention."

"It worked."

"It did." She was silent for a moment, then continued, "What are the chances that this'll work?"

"I have no idea," I said. "But if Elizabeth manages to protect Utopia, so much will change. Mira and I might not end up going to the Haven, which would mean we won't go to Moon Mountain, which means Hecate won't tell us how to find the Crown. Without the Crown, I won't become Queen of Pentacles. If that happens, Time will reject the change."

"But you don't know for sure if that'll happen."

"I don't. Which is why we're here, trying."

She nodded, satisfied, and together, we waited.

Soon enough, Queen Elizabeth burst into the room. Her skin paled when she saw us, like she was looking at ghosts.

She studied us for a few seconds, then said, "You both were in the meeting room practicing using your dragon magic. But you're also here."

"We are," I said.

"Who are you?"

"What do you mean?"

"It's impossible for anyone to duplicate themselves. So whoever the two of you are, you must have taken transformation potion to make yourselves look like Gemma and Harper."

I didn't answer.

Instead, I held my hands to my side and called on my dragon magic, creating an arc of fire above my head. Then I snuffed out the fire and held a hand out toward where a few crystals sat on the center of the kitchen table. I reached for them with my earth magic, and they floated up and toward us, until they hovered between us. I held them there for a few seconds, then returned them to where they'd been on the table.

"I'm the only person in the world with elemental dragon magic," I said. "Harper and I are both in the meeting room and in here with you."

"How?" she asked.

"Because I don't only have earth and fire magic." I reached into the ether, pulled out the Holy Crown, and placed it on my head. "I'm the Queen of Pentacles. And I can control the fifth element."

Her eyes widened as she gazed at the Crown. "What's the fifth element?" she asked.

"Time," I said. "The fifth element allows me to travel through time."

18

GEMMA

"Seriously?" She chuckled, then regained control of herself. "I've lived for over a thousand years. Longer than either of you could ever comprehend. I've heard a lot of stories in my days. But time travel... that's a new one."

"She's telling the truth," Harper said. "We came here from the future. That's why there are two versions of us."

"Impossible."

"I know it sounds crazy. It's easier if I show you." I held my hands out toward Queen Elizabeth. "Take my hands. It's not much different from teleporting."

She stared at my hands like they were covered in poison. "You want me to travel with you through time?"

"Is there any other way you'd believe me?"

"I don't trust it."

"I thought you didn't believe it was possible."

"Perhaps it's possible," she said. "But even if it is, it's not *natural*."

I held in a chuckle at the irony of the fact that this was being said by a supernatural vampire queen. Talk about *unnatural*.

"I'm the Queen of Pentacles," I repeated. "My magic is just as natural as the other three Queens.'"

She eyed the Crown, still not moving forward to take my hands.

I sighed at how difficult she was being, grabbed her hands, and thought, *Take us back to the present.*

I couldn't travel back in time when I was *already* back in time—I had to first return back to the present—so it was our only option.

We flickered out, then landed in the ransacked version of the apartment.

Queen Elizabeth looked around in shock. "What is this?" she asked.

"This is my present," I explained. "And *your* future."

She spun around to face me. "Why would anyone do this to your apartment?"

"It's not just my apartment," I said. "It's the entire kingdom. It's why I came back to find you. I need to tell you what happened so you can stop it."

She walked over to the door, opened it, and left the apartment. I followed her, and revulsion swirled through my stomach at the horrible sight in front of us.

The bridges that had connected the walls of the kingdom had collapsed and fallen to the bottom of the chamber, into the lake and onto the trees and restaurants on the ground floor. Doors had been broken into and left open. The crater at the top of the volcano had been blown open, allowing sunlight to stream into the silent, destroyed kingdom.

Elizabeth stood in the shadows, making sure the sun's rays didn't hit her. Then she turned around to face me, horror splattered across her face, and said, "I'm listening."

"I'll tell you everything," I said. "But I have to bring you back, and Harper and I can tell you there. We're on a bit of a time limit here in the present. Which won't be a problem if we explain in the past."

She stared at me like I'd lost my mind. "Okay," she said, and she walked forward and held her hands out, ready to leave.

I didn't take them. "I can't teleport, so we have to go back inside the apartment and leave from there," I explained. "Your guards are standing outside the door. It would alarm them if we appeared out of nowhere."

She walked back inside the apartment, saying nothing. When she turned back around to face me, she looked me up and down in approval. "I had a feeling that either you or Mira would become the final Queen," she said. "I'm glad it's you."

She held her hands out, and I brought us back to the past.

Harper was standing in the same place she'd been when we'd left, in the center of the room.

"How long were you gone?" she asked, since for her, it would have felt like a split second.

"Only a minute or two," I said. "Enough for her to see what happens."

Harper turned to Elizabeth with hope in her eyes. "You're going to stop it?"

"First, I need to know what 'it' is," she said, and we told her about the attack on Utopia, ending on her decision to remain in the throne room to face off against Lavinia and the demons, and how no one had seen her since.

She was silent as she took it all in.

"What happened after you left?" she asked. "How did you find the Crown and become the Queen of Pentacles?"

As quickly as possible, I told her about escaping to the Haven, going to Ember, finding the first half of the

Crown, and then going to Antarctica to find the second half.

"There is no Queen Katherine," she said once I was finished. "Only six of us did the spell to become original vampires."

"Queen Katherine says she was there," I said. "She said she was your friend."

"No compulsion can be that powerful," she said.

"It's her vampire gift," Harper repeated. "Superior compulsion."

"Then her compulsion would have to extend far enough to make everyone who'd ever heard her name so much as whispered by people passing by forget about her—to make them believe there was an entirely different past that this Katherine wasn't a part of," Elizabeth said. "Magic that strong is as dangerous as time travel."

"My magic isn't dangerous," I said. "I'm using it to try to save your kingdom."

"It *is* dangerous," she said. "Because if we change what happens, there's no saying how the future will turn out. It could change so drastically that you don't end up getting the Holy Crown. And, like you said, we need all four Queens to rise for a chance against the demons."

"Once a Queen has a Holy or Dark Object in my present, nothing I do can change that," I explained. "If I make a change that stops one of the Queens from rising, Time will reject the change."

She nodded in approval. "All magic needs limits," she said. "Now, tell me how you think I can save my kingdom."

19

GEMMA

We returned to the present, and Harper let out an anguished cry.

The apartment was a disaster. Everything was the same as when we'd left.

Disappointment filled me to the bones. Even though I'd had a gut feeling that the change would be too huge to stick, I'd *wanted* it to work.

Then I had another idea. One that might actually have a chance of working.

"Teleport me to the throne room," I told Harper.

Before Utopia had been ransacked, there'd been a spell around the kingdom that didn't allow teleportation inside. Now that the protection dome had been destroyed, so had that spell.

Harper took my hands and brought us to the throne room.

Luckily, any bodies that had remained after the battle had been cleared during the reconnaissance mission.

Everything else was in shambles.

Rocks that had broken off from the walls and ceiling covered the floor. The bridge that had connected the entrance to the area with the throne had collapsed into the crevice below. We stood next to the stump that remained of the throne, and the bones that had made up the dragon skull above it were broken and littered around the floor surrounding it.

The place where I'd created a tunnel in the wall had been sealed shut so cleanly that no one would have known the entrance had been there. Anything less, and I was sure Lavinia would have blasted through with the Dark Wand and chased us out.

"Why did you want to come here?" Harper asked.

"Hang tight," I said. "I'll be back in a second."

I flickered out before I could overthink it, and arrived in time to see the tunnel I'd forged in the wall close up.

Good job, past Gemma.

But I had no time to admire my handywork, because chaos surrounded me. Witches stood on guard, facing the only other way out of the chamber—the tunnel I'd collapsed to hold off the demons and dark witches. Bangs echoed from the other side of it, growing louder by the second.

It wouldn't be long until they broke through.

I spun to face the throne, where I knew Queen Elizabeth would be standing.

"Gemma," she greeted me, not looking surprised to see me.

It didn't make sense.

She'd *just* seen me leave the tunnel. Shouldn't she have been confused about how I'd appeared out of nowhere?

But we had no time to waste.

So I took her hands and reached for the Crown with my magic.

Take us back to the present.

We flickered out and landed in the destroyed throne room.

Harper's mouth dropped open when she saw us. "Your Highness?" she asked, as if she didn't believe Elizabeth was real.

Elizabeth surveyed the room. Then she focused on me, her expression grim. "Take me back," she said.

"No."

"I'm the Queen of Utopia. You will return me to my present, where I will fight with my people until the end."

"They're all going to die," I said. "You're going to go missing. There's nothing you can do to save them, or to save Utopia."

"Like you said, I'll be *missing*," she said, her eyes hard. "Not dead. Only a Nephilim can kill an original vampire. You have no idea what the version of myself in your present is doing."

"We assume you were taken by Lavinia," Harper said.

"And for all you know, the present version of me could be in Lilith's lair, working to beat the demons from the inside." She remained focused on me, tall and commanding. Anyone else would have cowered in her presence. But I was a Queen. Which meant we were equals. "Take me back. *Now*."

"How do you remember I can time travel?" I asked. "Time rejected the change we tried to make. For you, our visit in my apartment never would have happened."

She smirked knowingly. "As you said, Time would most likely have rejected the change if I'd attempted to change the future. So I had a witch create a memory potion for me. Before I drank it, I instructed her to give me the antidote this morning. The morning of the attack."

Harper clenched her fists in anger. "Why?"

"Because I wanted the future to play out as Fate intended—with Gemma finding the Holy Crown and becoming the Queen of Pentacles. I also wanted to remember everything you told me that day in the apartment, in case the knowledge came in handy later."

Harper's breathing quickened, her anger growing visibly. "You didn't even *try* to save our home?"

Elizabeth looked at her sadly, over a thousand years of wisdom shining in her gaze. "The future is what we make of it. But the past is set in stone," she said. "Anything else is unnatural. I have zero interest in messing around with Time."

"You're wrong," I said. "Fate *did* play out as intended—with me bringing you here safely."

"You speak of yourself like you're a god instead of a mortal."

"I'm not a god," I said. "But I *am* the Queen of Pentacles. The Holy Objects were created by the angels. I was gifted my magic to help us beat the demons, and we need the most powerful supernaturals fighting with us to do that. You may not trust my magic, but you don't have to. Because I'm asking you to trust *me*."

Harper moved to stand by my side. "As the Queen of Pentacles, Gemma outranks you," she said to Elizabeth. "If she feels this is the correct course of action, it's your responsibility to do as she commands."

"Is that what you're doing?" Elizabeth tilted her head, challenging me. "Are you *commanding* me?"

I exhaled and smiled slightly at such a ridiculous notion. "If you wish to return to when Lavinia attacked, I'll take you," I said, continuing before she could take me up on it. "However, it's only fair that I warn you—if you'd been successfully working behind the scenes to help us from Lilith's lair, I would have felt the timeline shift when we arrived back here. But I didn't. Which means you haven't done anything in Lilith's lair to change what's happening in the present. And while Lilith might not be able to kill you, there are fates worse than death. So I'm asking you to stay in this time and fight by our sides against the demons. Go wherever you choose—Avalon, the Haven, or the Tower for all I care. But I trust that you're strong enough and experienced enough to do as much good here as you could do there. Like you said, the future is what we make of it. So take this opportunity I've given you, and help us make our future a good one."

She was silent for a few seconds, her stone-cold expression betraying nothing.

"Well," she finally said. "Perhaps you have potential to be a strong Queen after all."

"Does that mean you'll stay?"

She paused, then smiled. "I've always been curious about what life is like on Avalon."

Joy raced through me, and I resisted the urge to jump up and hug her, since Queen Elizabeth wasn't the huggable type.

"Assuming you get through the Trials," Harper said.

"I'm a vampire queen." Elizabeth stood taller, looking every bit like the fierce warrior she was. "I'll pass the Trials."

"I thought I would, too," Harper muttered. "But life doesn't always turn out like we think it will."

"It sure doesn't," Elizabeth said. "And once we're in the Vale, I expect you to tell me how you seem to be both a witch *and* a vampire."

"When did you notice?" Harper asked.

"Back when the two of you spoke with me in Gemma's apartment. Did you really think the smell of *coffee* would cover up your vampire scent?"

"It was worth a try." She shrugged.

"It might have worked on someone with weaker senses," Elizabeth said. "But you should know I'm stronger than that."

"Of course." Harper lowered her eyes in apology. "We were short on time, so we couldn't come up with a better plan."

"Go figure. A time traveler short on time."

"My magic has limitations," I explained. "I'll tell you more about it later. But first, there's something else we still have to do here."

"What's that?" she asked.

I turned to Harper and said, "I hope you know where your mom was when Utopia was breached. Because I want you to take me there."

20

GEMMA

We stopped back in my apartment so I could change into clothes that I'd worn in Utopia, then Harper teleported us one at a time to the tunnel that led to what remained at the apothecary.

An entire magma chamber had been dedicated to the apothecary, where the most powerful witches in Utopia had created potions and spelled objects to use both inside the kingdom and for outside trade. Now, broken glass littered the floor, and the shelves had been swept clean.

We walked into the tunnel that led from the main cavern to the apothecary, since appearing in the shadows brought far less questions than popping into the center of a busy room.

"You shouldn't do this," Elizabeth warned. "You've

already messed with the past far more than you should have."

"I'm the Queen of Pentacles," I said. "And I can 'mess with the past' however I see fit."

I reached for my magic and connected it with the Crown. *Take me back to five minutes before Utopia's dome is breached*, I thought, and then I flickered out.

Someone walked into my shoulder with enough force to push me against the wall. A witch with brown hair and plain features who I hadn't met before.

"Sorry," she apologized, a hint of annoyance in her tone. "I didn't see you there."

Still facing the wall, I ripped the Crown off my head and stored it in the ether. Then I turned around and gave her a polite smile. "No worries. It happens."

Her mouth dropped open. "You're one of the twins."

"I'm Gemma," I said. "I'm here to speak with Tanya. Do you know where I can find her?"

"Probably at her station," she said, jittery, as if she was meeting a celebrity. "I'm Fiona—one of the assistants at the apothecary. I'll bring you there."

She walked me through the apothecary, which was brimming with life. Large potted plants sat on the floors, smaller ones were in the shelves alongside books, crystals and other witchy items, and others hung from the ceiling. They were all different colors and smelled like a variety of herbs. About ten large tables that reminded me of the ones from science classes at school were placed throughout the chamber, and a few witches stood at each one, brewing potions and casting spells on the crystals.

Fiona led me to a table in the center, where three witches were working. They were so consumed in their work that none of them glanced up.

"Where's Tanya?" she asked.

"She's making a delivery in the saloon," the silver-haired witch closest to her said, not looking up from the potion she was brewing.

"Tannen's?" I asked, recalling the name of the bar Benjamin had taken me to on our date.

That felt like it had been *forever* ago.

"The one and only."

"Thanks." With no time to waste, I spun around, ran out of the chamber and down the tunnel, and stopped at the first door I found—the entrance to one of the restaurants in the main cavern. I used my key and stepped into the Library's ivory hall. I didn't bother checking for Hecate before turning back around and opening the door again.

I entered the saloon through the swinging wooden doors and breathed out a sigh of relief when I saw Tanya sitting at the bar as the bartender—Clara—poured her some whiskey. Tanya looked like I imagined Harper would look in twenty-five years, if Harper hadn't been made immortal when she'd been turned into a vampire. Clara's boyfriend Emmett sat next to Tanya, examining the vials of potion she'd brought over. With his silver hair sticking out in all directions, he looked like some sort of mad scientist.

It was morning, and the bar was far from one of the most popular places in Utopia, so they were the only ones inside.

All of them looked to me when I entered.

"Gemma?" Tanya squinted, as if she wasn't seeing me correctly. "Aren't you supposed to be in the queen's chamber demonstrating your magic?"

"I am."

"So what are you doing here?"

"It's a long story, and I don't have time to explain." I hurried toward her, removed the Holy Crown from the ether, and placed it on my head. "Short version—I'm the Queen of Pentacles, and I'm here to save your life."

Tanya silenced at the sight of the Crown.

I grabbed her hands, and we flickered out and landed in the present.

The saloon wasn't in nearly as bad shape as my apartment and the apothecary. I supposed the demons weren't interested in whiskey. Even the glass Tanya had been drinking from still sat on the bar, nearly full, with dust covering its rim. The only signs that something bad had happened here were the upended tables and knocked-over chairs.

Tanya looked around in shock. "What's this?" she asked.

"I'll explain in a second," I said. "Be right back."

I flickered back to the moment after I'd left. Emmett and Clara were staring at the spot where Tanya and I had disappeared.

Clara hopped over the bar, fangs bared. "What did you do with her?" she asked.

"I saved her life. And I'm about to save yours, too."

I reached for her and brought her to the present, dropping her off next to Tanya. Then I went back and did the same for Emmett.

The three of them stood shoulder to shoulder, on guard, facing me.

"You said you'd explain in a second," said Tanya. "Now—explain."

"In about ten minutes, Lavinia was going to use the Dark Wand to break through Utopia's boundary dome," I said. "She, the demons, and other dark witches destroyed Utopia and everyone in it. By bringing you here, I saved your lives."

"Great Scott," Emmett said, his eyes wider than what

should have been physically possible. "Did you bring us into the future?"

"Forty-five days into the future, to be exact," I said. "Well, it's the future for *you*. It's my present."

Tanya walked over to the bar and picked up the glass she'd been drinking from earlier. She ran a finger over the dusty rim, then placed it back down. "How's it possible?" she asked.

"The Holy Crown gifted me with power over the fifth element," I said. "Time."

"Are you saying that the Holy Crown is a *time machine?*" Emmett asked.

"Sort of. I guess it's a time machine that only I can use. And it's not a machine. It's magic."

"How does it work? How far back can you go? Can you go to the future? How many people can—"

"I'll answer all your questions when I can." I held a hand up to stop him from asking more. "But we don't have time for that right now."

"You're a time traveler," he said. "Shouldn't you have all the time in the world?"

"You'd think. But it doesn't exactly work like that."

"You need to go back," Tanya said suddenly. "Harper was in the throne room. You need to rescue her, too."

"Harper's fine," I said. "A few of us escaped before Lavinia could get to us."

"How could you *escape?*" Tanya's eyes narrowed, skeptical. "There's only one way out of Utopia—through the top crater. The throne room is about as far from there as you can get."

"I used my earth magic to get us out. We went to the Haven, and Mary took us in. A lot's happened in the past forty-five days."

"Like you finding the Holy Crown and becoming the Queen of Pentacles."

"Yep."

"Forty-five days," Tanya repeated. "Harper thought I was gone that entire time."

"You *were* gone." I used the same terminology she had, since it sounded better than saying she'd been *dead*. "All three of you."

"Why did you save us?" Clara asked.

"I did it for Harper," I said. "And since the two of you were also there, I figured, why not?"

"Thank you." She bowed her head. "I'll be forever in your debt."

"Don't say that to a Queen," Tanya chided. "She might hold you to it."

"I saved you because I wanted to," I said. "None of you owe me anything. But Harper's waiting in the apothecary—"

Tanya ran out of the swinging doors before I could

finish my sentence, and she gasped at the sight of the ransacked city.

I followed behind her. "None of the spells that were around Utopia are still working," I said. "You can teleport to her. But first, you should know—"

She disappeared, cutting me off *again.*

Clara and Emmett joined me in the open hall.

"How are we supposed to get to the apothecary?" Clara asked. "The bridges are all destroyed, and I wouldn't trust the elevators, if they're still there. The only way out of here is by teleporting."

Of course, that wasn't true. But they wouldn't understand it if I told them my *special* way to get around.

"Wait here," I said, already reaching for the key around my neck. "I'll figure it out."

I walked back over to the swinging doors, stuck the key into a hole that didn't exist until the key was inches away from doors, and stepped into the Eternal Library.

21

GEMMA

Hecate wasn't there.

I stared at the door.

Where to from here?

I didn't want to interrupt Harper's reunion with her mom. They could teleport back to the Vale with Queen Elizabeth when they were ready.

But I needed to get Clara and Emmett to safety. And, given that Emmett was human, there was only one kingdom where he'd be safe.

First, I removed the Crown and put it back in the ether. Then I stepped back through the doors of the Library and into the tearoom at the Haven.

Raven stood in the center of the room, her arms crossed over her chest, looking furious. "Seriously?" she said when she saw me. "You're the Queen of Pentacles and you didn't tell me?"

Crap.

She was right.

"Sorry," I said. "Things have been crazy since getting back. Mira... well, she's missing."

"I know all about Mira and the Dark Crown," she said. "Mary caught me up on everything."

"She's the one who told you I'm the Queen of Pentacles."

"Nope. That was Genevieve. Who, by the way, looks an awful lot like her great-great-great whatever granddaughter, Geneva. I don't trust her. I know Geneva went out like a hero, but she was *not* one of the good guys. I know better than anyone, since I had the privilege of being kept prisoner by her for weeks."

"I know," I said, since I'd learned all about that in my studies about the Queens. "But Genevieve isn't Geneva. Did she tell you how I got the Holy Crown?"

"She told me everything," Raven said. "She introduced me to Queen Katherine, too. I don't trust either of them."

"I wouldn't have the Holy Crown if it wasn't for them."

"I still don't trust them."

I shrugged, since there was no point in arguing,

given how stubborn Raven was once she'd convinced herself of something.

"I can't stay for long," I said. "I need to get to Avalon."

"Took you long enough."

"I still need to go through the Angel Trials," I said. "But I just got back from a mission in Utopia. I need two witches to go there—to a bar called Tannen's Saloon. There's a vampire and a human waiting there who need to be teleported here."

"They've been surviving in the ruins for that long?"

"Not exactly." I pointed to my head, even though the Crown wasn't on it. "Time travel. Remember?"

"Time travel makes my head spin," she said.

"I went back to right before Lavinia attacked Utopia," I said, and I filled her in from there.

"I can get two witches to them," Raven said once I was done. "But first, can I see the Crown?"

"Of course." I pulled the Crown out of the ether and handed it to her.

She held it up to the light and studied it. "My mom will love this," she said. "She's into crystals and stuff. You'll meet her in Avalon."

"Assuming I pass the Angel Trials."

"You're one of the Holy Queens." She handed me back the Crown, and I placed it in the ether. "You'll pass."

I nodded, since I figured the same. I just didn't want to get too cocky about it, given what had happened to Harper.

"You *need* to pass," she continued. "So you can save Selena."

"Did you know her well?" I asked.

"I only knew her as Jacen and Annika's daughter, back when she had no magic. But she was a kid, so it wasn't like I hung out with her. Then, after she returned from the Otherworld, she disappeared to try to rescue Torrence. And we know how that ended. So I never got to know her after she became the Queen of Wands."

"After I fix this, you won't remember never knowing her," I said.

She frowned. "My memories will be erased?"

"Not erased," I said. "Another timeline will replace this one. A timeline where Selena didn't die. Everything from that moment on will be different."

"So I'll be a different person."

"You'll be the same." I had no way of knowing if that was true, but it was what I needed to say to make her comfortable, and I didn't want to get in a fight about this. "Your life will have been different these past few months, but everything that will happen in the new timeline will be real."

"And what happens to this timeline?"

"I think it disappears."

"You *think?*"

"I only got my magic recently." The days were blurring together, since time no longer passed the same way for me that it did for everyone else. "I don't have all the answers about how it works."

Add "what happens to the previous timelines" to the list of questions for Hecate, I thought.

"But Selena will be alive," I continued. "And that's what matters."

"Yes," she said, although she bit her lower lip, still looking troubled. "I suppose so."

"Anyway, I need to get back to the Vale," I said. "Sorry I couldn't stay long. King Alexander and Queen Deidre are insisting on having dinner with me, Ethan, and my mom before we enter the Angel Trials. You'll send those witches to Utopia?"

"On it," she said. "Then I'm getting back to Avalon. I'll be waiting for you on the dock when you arrive." She paused, then asked, "How are you getting back to the Vale?"

"I have my ways," I said, and then I reached for my key, stepped through the door, and entered Hecate's Eternal Library.

Hecate wasn't there, so I turned around and went

back to the Vale. Since I'd been in Harper's room when I'd left, that was where I arrived.

Harper, Tanya, and Elizabeth were all there. Harper's eyes were rimmed with red—she'd been crying.

"Where did you go?" she asked.

"The Haven," I said. "They're sending witches to bring Clara and Emmett there."

"Good." Tanya nodded. "That'll be a good place for them to stay."

"So…" I took a deep breath and looked around at the group. "I guess I'm going to have to tell the others that I went back in time and saved your lives."

"Don't look so worried," Elizabeth said. "You're a Queen. You don't need permission to do anything."

"Weren't you just telling me that you think my power's unnatural?"

"I still think that," she said. "But it's yours to use how you see fit. Don't let the others control you. Make sure not to lose their respect."

"I won't," I said. "But like you said—I'm a Queen. I'm going to be working *with* the other Queens. I'll try to run it by them before I make any big changes to history."

Except that they won't know when I make changes. Maybe there will be things they don't need to know?

I'd deal with it later.

"You're going to make a great Queen," Harper said. "I can feel it."

"I hope so."

"Where's Queen Deidre?" Elizabeth asked. "I should make my arrival in her kingdom known as soon as possible."

"It's not just her kingdom," Harper said. "It's King Alexander's, too."

"Of course." Elizabeth brushed it off, clearly not wanting to acknowledge the male supernatural who also ruled the Vale.

"They're giving my mom and Ethan a tour," I said, and my chest tightened the moment I said Ethan's name.

He was *not* going to be happy when he learned that I went back to Utopia and traveled back in time without him.

But like Elizabeth had said, *I* was the Queen of Pentacles. And while I did intend to work with the other Queens, I didn't need permission to use my power.

"Let's head to the throne room," Harper said. "I'll send the king and queen a fire message to have them meet us there."

22

GEMMA

As expected, Ethan was *not* happy when he heard about my side trip to Utopia.

"What were you *thinking?*" he said for the third time. "You could have died."

I didn't bother responding, since I'd already told him that I'd been thinking that I could save lives—and that I'd succeeded.

"Let's consider it a warm-up for saving Selena," Harper said.

Ethan glared at me. "You should have taken me with you."

"You would have tried to convince me not to go," I said. "We didn't have time for that."

"Enough," Elizabeth said. "What's done is done. Gemma saved me—the Queen of Utopia. She should be rewarded for her actions, not chided. She's the Queen of Pentacles. She needs permission from no one to use her magic."

"She's my twin flame," Ethan said, and chills ran up and down my arms when he said it. *Excited* chills. He turned to me and continued, "Promise me you'll let me know before you do something like that again."

"I can't do that."

"Why not?"

"Because there's no saying where I'll be when I need to travel."

He sucked in a long breath, exhaling slowly as he gathered his thoughts. "Then promise me you'll try."

I pressed my lips together, saying nothing.

"The two of you can continue this conversation in private," Queen Deidre said, her stern tone making it clear that she didn't have time to listen to our quarrel. "Elizabeth and Tanya—would you also like to try to go to Avalon?"

"Yes," Elizabeth said.

"No." Tanya stood proudly next to Harper. "I'm staying with my daughter."

"Very well," said Deidre. "Dinner will be ready soon. There's much we want to learn from Gemma before her departure to Avalon. Let's eat, and then we'll send you on your way."

We filled the others in on everything during the multi-course meal. They were interested in how my magic worked, and I told them everything I knew.

"How do you know that eating the mana will heal the Crown and allow you to travel further back in the past?" Deidre asked.

"I went to Hecate's Eternal Library. She looked up my question and gave me the answer."

Queen Deidre blinked, then smiled blankly. "Wonderful," she said. "I'm happy to hear you have that covered."

Harper smirked at how easily what I'd said had been accepted by the queen.

"Do they truly not have actual food on Avalon?" Mom asked after we finished dessert.

"That's what those who have been there say," Deidre said. "The mana tastes like any food you desire."

"So there's no need to cook."

"Avalon's focus is on training warriors," Elizabeth said. "The fewer other tasks to focus on, the better."

Mom frowned, clearly troubled. I understood why—one of her greatest passions in life was baking the pastries in the café. She loved creating new recipes. Baking had been her job in Utopia, too.

A life without baking would be the same thing to her as a life without reading would be to me.

Meaning, it would be totally and completely unacceptable.

"You're welcome to stay the night," Deidre said once we'd finished the meal. "However, I understand if you want to start the Angel Trials as soon as possible. I assume you're anxious to get to Avalon."

"We are," I said, although I glanced at Harper, sad to be leaving her again.

"We'll see each other again soon," she promised.

"How do you know that?"

"I just do."

I smiled, since I knew what witch intuition felt like. Plus, I eventually expected an update from her about the location of the Dark Sword.

"Also, now you've been to the Vale," she continued. "You can use your key to visit whenever you want. Just don't come *straight* into my room. I'd appreciate if you knocked first."

Pink crept into her cheeks, and I had a feeling I knew what she was thinking—she didn't want me walking in on her and Rohan.

As always when we mentioned the keys, it was like the others hadn't heard anything she'd said.

"I'll call for Prince Rohan now," Deidre said. "And he'll take you straight to the start of the Trials."

Rohan entered the room, and Harper jumped in to letting him know how we'd saved her mom and Elizabeth.

"I have so much to catch my mom up on about what's happened since I got to the Vale," she said, and the undertone was clear—she didn't want Rohan acting familiar with her until she had a chance to tell her mom about him.

Knowing how the women of Utopia viewed supernatural men, I knew that wasn't going to be an easy conversation. But hopefully her mom would come around and be as happy for Harper as I was.

Rohan escorted me, Ethan, Mom, and Elizabeth down the dark, spiral staircase and to the portal that led to the start of the Angel Trials. Elizabeth stayed as far away from Rohan as possible, as if his pores leaked poison.

"This is where I leave you," he said. "I wish you the best of luck."

"Thanks," I said, and I looked nervously to my mom.

"Don't worry about me." She smiled, pride shining in

her eyes. "The Haven has felt like home to me ever since we arrived. If I fail the Trials, I'll return there."

"You're not going to fail the Trials," I said, although the words felt hollow as I spoke them.

"I'm going to try my hardest," she said. "But if I don't pass, then you know where to find me."

I nodded, since I trusted she'd be safe in the Haven. Plus, with the key, I'd be able to visit her whenever I wanted.

I faced the glowing portal and took a deep breath, knowing so much was at stake once I started the Trials.

"Can we go through together?" I asked Rohan.

"One by one," he said. "Who wants to go first?"

"Me," Ethan said, and before any of us could argue, he stepped through the portal, and was gone.

I knew why he'd done it—he didn't want me being on the other side without him there to protect me.

Elizabeth went through next, then my mom, and then I stepped through the bright, glowing light, ready to face whatever waited on the other side.

23

GEMMA

When I awoke, I felt like I was waking up from being knocked out with tranquilizer. My body felt heavy, and my lids didn't want to open. Sunlight bathed me with warmth, calming me so I didn't panic.

Flashes of a dream passed through my mind—a beach surrounded by cliffs, a cave, rolling hills, a dark forest, and a castle in the sky. I'd done something in all those places, but I couldn't remember exactly *what* I'd done. The more I came to, the more the dreams slipped away.

From the light rocking motion, I could tell that I was in some sort of boat. My stomach cramped with nausea, and I groaned. The rocking was barely there, but even that was enough to affect my motion sickness.

The heaviness left my body, and I opened my eyes and pushed myself up.

I was in a rowboat, floating toward a cove of bright blue water. An island with mountains covered with lush greenery surrounded the cove. Puffy white clouds filled the sunny sky, and it was that perfect temperature where you couldn't feel the weather.

Queen Elizabeth was in an identical boat ahead of me, and Ethan was in one behind me. Both of them looked dazed, as if they'd both also woken up from a heavy sleep.

Ethan pulled off the bedhead look like he was a male model getting ready for a photoshoot. But I barely paid him any attention. Because Mom wasn't there. I twisted around, searching for another boat with her in it, but there was no sign of one.

I'd known there was a chance she wouldn't make it to Avalon. I'd tried to prepare myself for it. But I'd wanted to be wrong.

Any hope that Avalon might be a place I'd call home vanished. How could I feel at home in a place my mom couldn't visit?

The boat drifted into an inlet, now so close to Elizabeth and Ethan's boats that the front and back of mine nearly touched theirs. It was like we were on a ride in an amusement park.

Bright green grass grew on both sides of the inlet, and trees with strange white fruit dangling from their thick branches lined the fields. Fae with bright, sparkling wings hung around the trees, picking the fruit and placing it in woven baskets.

At the sight of us, the fae rushed forward and gathered by the riverbank. They frowned as we floated by, then turned around and resumed their jobs of picking the fruit from the trees.

"Don't look too happy to see us," Elizabeth muttered.

As we moved down the river, the fae continued to run to get a good look at us. All of them were disappointed when they got a good view.

"You okay?" Ethan asked from behind me.

I didn't need to ask to know he was referring to the fact that my mom wasn't with us.

"I'm fine," I lied.

We turned around a corner, into a tunnel carved into one of the tallest mountains. Water dripped from the stone, and fire lit the torches along the walls. It should have felt ominous, but somehow, it didn't.

We must have been deep inside the mountain when we turned another corner and floated toward a dock. As promised, Raven waited for us on it. A broad-shouldered man with shaggy brown hair stood next to her, holding her hand. Raven looked up at him and smiled. She seemed happier than I'd ever seen her.

Our boats stopped at the dock, lined up with the fronts of them touching it.

"Congrats on passing the Angel Trials," Raven said. "Welcome to Avalon."

"Thank you." Queen Elizabeth stepped out of her boat and onto the dock with no hesitation. The shrunken heads around her belt rustled against each other, and while the man standing next to Raven glanced at them, he didn't acknowledge them beyond that.

Ethan also stepped out of his boat, then he turned around and offered me his hand.

I took it on instinct, and his grip tightened around mine as he helped me out, as if he was worried I'd pull away.

Which was exactly what I did the moment both of my feet were on the dock.

He frowned, but said nothing.

The warmth that had rushed through me at his touch disappeared. Instinct urged me to reach for his hand again, but I resisted.

"I'd like to introduce you to my mate." Raven smiled again at the man next to her, then refocused on us. "This is Noah."

"Welcome," he said simply.

"This is Queen Elizabeth of Utopia," Raven continued the introductions. "King Ethan Pendragon of Ember. And the Queen of Pentacles, Gemma Brown."

"Good thing I'm getting used to being surrounded by royalty," Noah said, sharing another knowing look with Raven.

It was like the two of them could read each other's minds.

Then I remembered what I'd learned about shifters and their mate bonds. They felt each other's feelings and could *actually* send thoughts to one another.

I was grateful that dragons were an entirely different species than the shifters on Earth. My feelings for Ethan were too intense and confusing for even me to handle. I did *not* want to share my emotions and thoughts with him.

"You're basically royalty yourself, being the alpha of our pack and all," Raven said.

He shrugged, as if being a pack alpha didn't mean much to him.

"Sorry about your mom," Raven said to me. "She'll be well taken care of in the Vale."

"She's going back to the Haven," I said.

"She fits in nicely there."

"She does."

"What do you remember of the Trials?" Raven asked.

I pressed my lips together and tilted my head as I searched through my memories. I knew I'd remembered a bit when I'd first woken up, but now it was fuzzy.

"Nothing," I said, and Ethan and Elizabeth agreed.

"We don't remember much from our Trials, either," Raven said. "No one else has ever remembered anything. But I always ask, just in case."

"How long were we gone?" Ethan asked.

"Only a day. Sometimes the Trials are longer, sometimes shorter. Yours was on the shorter end."

One day. Which meant it was now five days since Mira went missing. Well, five days in the present. Because of my time traveling, I'd lived more than five days during that time. But my mind was spinning far too much by this point to attempt to calculate exactly how much time had passed for me since I'd received my time travel ability.

"The fae watched us as we sailed in," Elizabeth said. "Why?"

"As you know, the Otherworld has been destroyed by the infected fae," Raven said. "The Nephilim are doing our best to search the Otherworld and rescue any fae or half-bloods that have been hiding out. From there, the fae have been entering the Angel Trials. Whenever newcomers come in, the fae hope to see the faces of family and friends who went missing in the Otherworld."

"Which explains why they looked disappointed to see us," Elizabeth said.

"Exactly," she said. "Anyway, Annika wants me to bring Gemma and Ethan to her as soon as possible. Elizabeth, you'll be going with Noah. He'll take you to orientation."

Elizabeth looked at Noah and frowned. "I'll be going with a wolf." The name of his species sounded like a dirty word when she said it.

"I don't bite." Noah smirked. "At least, not when unprovoked."

Raven gave him a warning glare. "We have no prejudices on Avalon," she said to Elizabeth. "All species—and genders—are treated equally. Will that be a problem for you?"

Elizabeth paused, and I worried she was going to say yes and turn around.

"I suppose I'll have to learn to deal with it," she said instead.

"Given that you passed the Angel Trials, I'm sure you'll be able to adjust," Raven said. "Your first chance to do that is now, with Noah. The mages are waiting for you in the orientation room so they can answer as many of your questions as possible."

"I'll have many," she said.

"I expected no less." Raven let go of Noah's hand, gave him a quick kiss, and then Noah took Elizabeth up winding stone steps to the right.

"She's tough," Raven said once they were gone. "Good call rescuing her from Utopia. She'll make a fantastic addition to Avalon's army."

"It was a dangerous call to go back and save her, given that it was during Lavinia's attack," Ethan said.

"Danger is part of being a Queen," Raven said. "It took Noah some time to get used to my running into danger, too. But I was always destined to become the Queen of Swords. He knows I can handle my job."

"Selena was destined to become a Queen, too," Ethan said. "And look how that ended up for her."

We all silenced at the reminder of Selena's death.

"It's going to end up fine for her," I said. "Because we're going to save her."

"Yes, you are." Raven forced brightness into her tone that sounded like desperate hope more than true faith. "Now, come with me. Because there's someone you need to meet."

24

GEMMA

RAVEN BROUGHT us up another set of steps that led into the first floor of what looked like a medieval castle. The halls were huge, with wood floors and giant tapestries hanging on the stone walls.

I would have thought we'd traveled back in time, if it wasn't for the everyday clothing and black Avalon Army jumpsuits worn by the people passing by. They parted to the sides to make way for Raven, watching me and Ethan with curiosity and excitement.

Raven led us up more stairs, to an empty hall on the third floor. We walked all the way to the end, and she knocked on a huge, rounded door.

A woman with hair the same shade of red as Raven's entered. Their features were so similar that it was clear she was Raven's mother.

Skylar Danvers. The vampire prophetess who could use tarot cards to see the future.

"This is my mom," Raven said what I'd already guessed. "Mom, this is Gemma and Ethan."

We all said hello, and then Raven's mom opened the door more for us to come in. We turned into a living room where two people waited on a sofa across from a fireplace. The man was a vampire with dark hair and strong features, and the woman had long brown hair and golden eyes. There were circles under both of their eyes—they looked worn out and exhausted.

Since only angels had completely golden eyes, she had to be the Earth Angel—the Queen of Cups, Annika Pearce. I assumed the vampire sitting next to her was her husband, Jacen.

They stood when they saw us, and when her golden eyes met mine, hope flickered through them.

Without any warning, she ran toward me and engulfed me in a huge hug.

"Is it true?" she asked when she pulled back, her eyes glazed with tears. "You can save Selena?"

"I'll do my absolute best," I promised.

She nodded, as if she had no doubt that my "absolute best" meant Selena would be saved.

The man walked forward to stand by her side. "I'm Jacen," he introduced himself. "This is my wife, Annika."

"Hi," I said. "I'm Gemma."

"And I'm Ethan," he said. "The King of Ember."

"Thank you for protecting Gemma all this time," said Annika.

"I'd do anything to keep her safe."

I stilled at how *sure* he sounded. And I knew he meant it. So why hadn't he been honest with me and Mira from the start? It would have saved us both an incredible amount of heartbreak.

"Where's the Holy Crown?" Jacen asked.

"Oh, right." I pulled it out of the ether and placed it on my head. I was always surprised by how light and comfortable it was.

"It doesn't look broken," he said.

"It was split into two when we found it. Even though it was welded together, it's apparently still broken on the inside."

"Mary filled us in on everything," Annika said. "We have mana ready for you so you can fix the Crown."

She led the way to the small dining table. It looked like it would comfortably seat four people, but it had six chairs crowded around it. The glasses of water were full, and a dish of the strange white fruit I'd seen growing from Avalon's trees sat in the center of the table.

Annika sat down first, and the rest of us followed.

She motioned to the white fruit. "Help yourself."

I reached for a piece of fruit—it was about the size of a mango—and placed it on my plate.

They all watched me expectantly. None of them took a piece of their own.

Was I supposed to pick it up and take a bite, or use a fork and knife?

Since there were place settings, I picked up the fork and knife, cut into it, and took a bite.

It tasted like my favorite grilled cheese sandwich from the café—butter, grease, and all.

I ate until the fruit was gone. No one else was eating—they all watched me, like they were waiting for me to sprout wings or grow a second head at any moment.

I didn't sprout wings. Or grow a second head. But warmth filled my body, my head tingled, and white light glowed through the room.

It came from the Crown.

The light eventually died down, and the Crown buzzed with energy unlike I'd ever felt from it before.

Annika leaned forward eagerly. "Well?"

"I think it worked," I said.

"You *think*?"

"I'd have to test it out to know for sure."

"All right." She gazed out the window at the lush fields and mountains, then turned back to me. "Seventeen years ago, Jacen and I came to Avalon for the first time. Go back to before then and tell us what you see."

I closed my eyes and thought, *Take me back to a few days before Annika and Jacen arrived on Avalon.*

I opened my eyes in time to see the room flicker out around me—and to see Ethan's angry gaze. He reached for me, but I was gone before he could touch me.

The tapestries on the walls disappeared, and I fell through the chair, my butt hitting the cold stone floor.

"Ow," I said, even though no one was there to hear me.

I stood and looked around, rubbing my tail bone to ease the pain. I'd fallen onto the floor because there *was* no chair. There was no furniture at all. It was just a cold, empty room—a ruined castle. The fireplace was caved in. A gaping space remained where the door had been, leading out into the equally ruined hall. It smelled musty, and a nearly suffocating humidity blanketed my skin.

I walked to the window and looked outside. Gone were the lush fields and mountains. The trees and grass were brown and dead. The overcast sky let no sunshine through, and the water in the cove was dark, murky blue. There were no signs of life anywhere.

It was like I'd gone back centuries—not seventeen years.

But the Crown always listened to my instructions. Which meant Avalon had been in shambles before Annika and Jacen had arrived.

Or maybe, now that I'd eaten the mana, the Crown was too powerful for me to handle. Maybe it *had* taken me back centuries.

I shivered at the possibility.

Take me back to the present, I thought, and the dead island flickered out, replaced by the lush, sunny place I'd originally arrived. The uncomfortable humidity disappeared, and I could breathe again.

I spun around, glad to find the room furnished as before, with a welcoming fire in the mantle. It burned taller at my presence.

The others watched me expectantly. Only a split second had passed for them, so it had appeared like I'd teleported from sitting at the chair to standing by the window.

Ethan stood and gripped the back of his chair. "You should have taken me with you."

"I was fine," I snapped, since after everything he'd done to me, I had zero need or desire to defend my actions to him.

The fire crackled, like it was reacting to the anger inside him. Or inside me. Or both.

"What did you see?" Annika asked.

"It worked," I said. "But either Avalon was in complete ruins right before you arrived, or the Crown accidentally took me back centuries."

She sighed in relief. "Avalon was dead when we first got here," she said.

"How did it change so quickly?"

"When I arrived, I signed a contract, promising myself as the leader of Avalon," she said. "I signed it with my blood. Immediately after the contract was signed, the island bloomed with life, and the castle restored itself. But all magic comes from somewhere. By using my blood to revitalize Avalon, I bound myself to the island. My life force is the heart of the island—it's what keeps Avalon alive. It's why I can never leave."

"What would happen if you tried?"

"I'd be breaking the contract, and Avalon would revert to the way it was before I'd arrived."

I nodded, feeling bad for her. Avalon was paradise, but in a way, it was also Annika's prison.

"Don't look so sad," she said. "I knew what I was getting into when I signed the contract. I'm blessed to provide a safe place for the supernaturals that's safe from the demons. A place that allows us to be the best versions of us we can be. But without Selena here…" She shrugged and trailed off, then snapped back to attention. "It doesn't matter. Because now that you can travel back further than the past few months, you can save her and bring her home."

"I'm going to do my absolute best," I reminded her. "But to do that, I'll need help."

"I'll give you anything you need."

"Then I need you to send for Torrence. Because if anyone can help me strategize about how to save Selena, it's her best friend."

25

GEMMA

We spent the rest of the day brainstorming. The tricky part was that we had to figure out the *exact* right time to travel back to, and the right way to do it, to make as little impact on anything else in the future.

There were a few possibilities, but Torrence was adamant about which one she thought would work the best. So we decided to trust her judgement.

Eventually, we grew so tired that we were going over the same things over and over again without being productive. So we called it a night.

Annika looked warily between me and Ethan. "Do the two of you want shared quarters?"

"No," I said, even though the thought of sharing a bed with Ethan caused a pleasant warmth to bloom in my stomach.

Life would be so much easier if the mere thought of him didn't make my body react the way it did.

"I'd like our rooms to be next to one another," Ethan said.

"No problem," Annika said, and she showed Ethan to the room across from hers, and me to the one next to his. He walked with us as she showed me my room, making sure our rooms were as close as possible. "There are clothes in the wardrobes—enough sizes that you'll be able to find things that fit—and the bathrooms are stocked with all the necessities," Annika said. "Is there anything else I can get you?"

"This is great," I said, since the rooms were fit for royalty. "Thanks."

"See you tomorrow."

"See you." I walked inside and closed the door before Ethan had a chance to say anything to me.

I took a quick shower, changed into the world's most comfortable pajamas, used my magic to light the fireplace, then collapsed into the king-sized, canopy bed. I tossed the decorative pillows to the floor, snuggled under the thick comforter, and started to drift asleep to the soothing sound of the fire crackling.

Then the door creaked open.

Not the door leading to the hall, but the one to my bathroom.

My eyes snapped open, and I watched Ethan step through.

That was why he'd wanted to check out my room.

He wanted to be able to use his key to get inside.

Quickly, I closed my eyes and rolled over. If I pretended to already be asleep, maybe he wouldn't bother me.

"Gemma," he said softly. "I know you're awake."

I rolled over, sighed, and opened my eyes. He was standing next to my bed, watching me, waiting for me to react.

"What do you want?" I asked.

"You've been ignoring me for days," he said. "We need to talk."

"I don't want to talk. I need to sleep."

"And I need you to hear me out."

Anger rushed through me at his insistent tone, and I pushed myself up in bed, no longer tired. "We have a long day tomorrow, and I need to sleep to make sure I'm as alert as possible," I said. "Unless you don't care if demons capture me, like they did with Mira?"

I regretted the words the moment they came out of my mouth, especially given his pained expression.

"Sorry," I said. "I didn't mean that."

"I know." He tentatively moved forward and sat on the edge of the bed, leaving about a meter between the two of us. "But you have every right to hate me after what happened."

"I don't *hate* you," I said. "I'm just…" I paused, searching for a way to express the inner turmoil that had been storming inside me ever since Mira had attacked me with her magic and left the Seventh Kingdom. "We need to get her back."

"We will," he said, even though there was no way he could promise that. Still, it helped to know that he believed it was possible.

"I'm not ready to talk about what happened," I said. "We have to focus on saving Selena. To do that, I need sleep."

"You're a time traveler," he said. "We can go back in time, get as much sleep as we need, then come back fully rested. There's no reason to be deprived of sleep ever again."

"I know." I'd already thought of that. I just wanted him out of my room before he could launch into a conversation where he tried to get me to understand why he'd lied to me and Mira.

Deep down, I wanted to understand why he'd done it more than anything. He was my twin flame. I wanted to let him in, to love him fully and completely.

But what if his explanation wasn't good enough? What if I could never forgive him?

The possibility of having to reject the one person in this world who was supposed to be my perfect match tore at my soul so much that I could barely breathe.

"What I need from you now can't wait," he said.

I sat completely still, forcing myself to breathe steadily to calm the frantic beating of my heart.

I didn't think I'd ever be ready for this conversation. But I was going to have to face what had happened, one way or the other.

It might as well be now.

"Okay." I braced myself for whatever he might throw my way, even though I couldn't imagine an explanation that could justify his actions.

"I want to go back in time and save my father."

"What?" I blinked, caught off-guard by his request.

"You saved Queen Elizabeth, and you saved Harper's mom," he said. "I know it's a long shot, but I have to try to save my dad."

"It's more than a long shot," I said. "If we save your dad, Lavinia won't find the Dark Wand or the Dark Crown. She and Mira won't become Queens. There's no way Time will accept the change."

"We don't know that for sure," he said. "Lavinia might find another way to track down the Dark Objects."

"Maybe," I said, even though it was highly unlikely.

By the look on Ethan's face, he knew it, too.

"I know you don't owe me anything, especially after all that's happened," he said, desperation creeping into his tone. "But if I don't try to save him, I'll never be able to live with myself."

I nodded, since I understood completely. If Mira or Mom had been the ones who'd been killed, I'd try anything to save them. I'd keep trying until so much time passed for me in the past that I was too old and frail in the present to continue trying. I'd try until I either succeeded or died.

Ethan was right—I didn't *owe* him anything.

But I wanted to give him this. If I didn't, I wouldn't be able to live with myself, either.

"Of course we can try," I said, and he released all the tension he'd been holding in his body. "But if we save him, and then Time rejects the change, you realize it's out of my power to do anything more. Right?"

"I do," he said, and then he added, "Thank you."

We held each other's gazes for a few seconds, neither of us moving. Tension crackled between us, and it took every cell in my body to resist moving toward him.

"So," I said, breaking the spell in the air. "I'm guessing you have a plan?"

"I always have a plan," he said, and from there, he told me how he wanted to try to save his father.

26

GEMMA

We'd been up for far too long and were too exhausted to get much of anything done. So the first part of the plan was to get some sleep. But not in the present, since we'd be waking up in a few hours to start our mission to save Selena. Instead, we used our keys to go to the Haven.

As always, we checked to see if Hecate was in the Library. Like most times, she wasn't. So we entered the tearoom, I took Ethan's hands, and transported us back to the moment after we'd left for the Vale.

Mary was the only one there. She looked at us and smiled. "You've come from the future," she said simply.

"Yes," I said, and I briefed her on everything that had happened since we'd left for the Vale. "We need to crash here for a bit. Is that okay?"

"You're the Queen of Pentacles," she said. "You have a right to 'crash here' whenever you need."

I nodded, since I'd expected as much. Still, this was her kingdom, and it felt polite to ask. "We'll be in our rooms," I said. "Make sure they're still empty in my current present, since we'll need to pop back there before traveling to the past again."

"Consider those rooms permanently yours," she said. "I'll make sure to never give them to any other guests, so they'll be at your disposal whenever you need to catch up on sleep."

"Thank you."

We used our keys to go to our rooms, and Ethan didn't even try to stay in the room with me. Relief passed through me at his respect of that boundary of mine, and I fell into a deep slumber after my head touched the pillow.

I slept for nine hours straight, then changed into my Haven whites. Ethan was already awake when I knocked on the door that connected his room to mine, also dressed in his clothes from the Haven.

"You look rested," he said.

"I feel it," I said, surprised that after everything we'd been through, it was true. I suspected it was because of the mana and holy water we'd had on Avalon, which provided our bodies with every nutrient they needed to function at their best capacity.

Speaking of food, I was starving. I sent Mary a fire message, and she had breakfast delivered to our rooms in less than ten minutes.

"You ready?" I asked Ethan after we finished eating.

"As ever," he said, and then I took his hands and brought us back to the present. From there, we used our keys to head over to his house in Australia.

It was empty. No one had been there since we'd left, and dust had gathered on all the surfaces.

It felt like so long ago that we'd sat at that dining room table with Mom, Mira, and Rosella and learned about the existence of the supernatural world.

"Glad to see the demons didn't rampage the place," Ethan said, and I nodded, since that was one thing so far working in our favor.

He led me up to his room, which I was extremely familiar with, thanks to the memories I'd experienced of the other life I'd had with him. The huge television, gaming station, and shelf full of books were in the same places I remembered.

"Don't get distracted by the bookshelf," he warned, with a hint of playfulness in his tone.

I couldn't help but smile back. "It's difficult to resist. But I think I can manage a bit of self-control. Barely."

Especially since I already knew exactly what books he owned, and which ones were his favorites. I'd looked through that shelf more times than I could count.

Of course, he didn't know that.

Since he didn't know *me*.

I pushed down the pain that came along with the unwelcome reminder.

"We need to go back to the day before the start of Christmas break," Ethan reminded me.

I connected with the Crown's magic, took his hands, and we flickered out. The next moment, the light shined at a different angle through the window, the bed was unmade, and dust no longer covered all the surfaces.

From the fresh smell of soap coming from the connected bathroom, Ethan had showered that morning before heading out to school. And, only a few kilometers away, Mira and I were walking through the halls, heading to our first class of the day.

It had been one of the last days my twin had felt truly happy.

Even if we saved her—no, *when* we saved her—I'd never have that carefree version of her back. I was sure that what had happened to her had changed her beyond repair.

"Gemma," Ethan said, concerned. "You okay?"

"Yeah," I lied. "It's just strange to be back here."

"I know." From the look in his eyes, I could tell he felt it, too. The stillness in the air of what felt like the calm before the storm.

But it had to be a hundred times worse for him. Because if his assumption was correct, his dad was downstairs, unaware that in a few days, his life was going to be cut short.

I reached for the Crown, ready to put it in the ether.

"Keep it on," Ethan said. "We need proof that we're telling the truth."

"Right," I said, and I placed the Crown back on my head. We'd already discussed that part of the plan, but taking the Crown off when I wasn't using it felt natural. Which was a good thing... except when I needed to prove I was a Holy Queen who'd traveled back in time to share knowledge of the future.

"Let's do this," he said, and then together, we walked down the stairs... where we found his dad and Rosella sitting in the living room with four cups of coffee in front of them, as if they were ready to receive guests.

27

GEMMA

Ethan froze and stared at his dad in shock.

I couldn't imagine what this might be like for him. For the past few weeks, he'd believed his dad was dead. And his dad *had* been dead. But now here he was, very much alive, and apparently expecting guests.

"I've been waiting for this moment ever since bringing you and your sister out of Ember," his dad said, and he motioned to the empty seats. "Please, sit."

I eyed Rosella as we walked toward the couches. She sat straight, her blank eyes revealing nothing.

How did she know we were coming? Yes, she had future sight, but she could only see the future as it was in the current moment. She couldn't see changes I made in the timeline until I'd actually traveled back in time. Which meant that years ago—when Ethan's dad had brought him and his sister out of Ember—she shouldn't have known about this visit Ethan and I were paying them now.

Ethan sat on the couch next to his dad, although he left some space between them. It was like he was afraid that if he got too close, this would stop being real.

I took the chair that faced Rosella.

"You knew we were coming?" Ethan asked his dad.

"Yes."

"How?"

"Prince Devyn," Ethan's dad said the name of Selena's biological dad—the only known fae gifted with omniscient sight. "Haven't you ever wondered how I got the portal tokens that allowed me to take you and your sister out of Ember?"

"Of course I've wondered," Ethan said. "I figured that when you were ready to tell me—*if* you were ever ready to tell me—you would."

"Now's that time," he said. "When Prince Devyn found me in Ember and gave me the portal tokens, he told me that the future depended on getting you and your sister to Earth. I wasn't happy about it—I had a kingdom to rule—but after consulting my advisors, we agreed it was for the best. Especially since I was able to return to Ember whenever I pleased."

He reached for the chain around his neck and pulled

one of Hecate's keys out from under his shirt. His key was shaped like a sword, with a dragon wrapped around the body. Green jewels inlayed the top three points of the sword.

"I thought you might have a key," Ethan said. "But how?"

"As you also might have figured out by now, our family line has a small amount of witch blood in it—back from the short time dragons were on Earth," his dad said. "It's enough that we're able to reach Hecate's Eternal Library if we pass her trials on Moon Mountain. The kings of Ember have received keys from Hecate for generations. It's how we've kept what remains of our people safe from the Dark Allies, and how we've pulled off a few rescue missions during that time."

I glanced at Rosella, who was sipping her coffee so casually that it was like she wasn't hearing a word of what Ethan's dad was saying.

She probably *wasn't* hearing what he was saying, since she didn't have a key.

"Due to the nature of the key—the way we can only visit places we've already been—I wasn't able to go to Earth until getting the portal tokens and going to Earth myself," Ethan's dad continued. "After that point, I was able to take care of both my kingdom *and* my children." He looked at Ethan proudly—and sadly. "I'm sure you're making a wonderful king. Our people are lucky to have you as their ruler."

Ethan's jaw clenched. "You know?"

"Yes," his dad confirmed. "When Prince Devyn gave me the portal tokens, he told me that sometime in the future, my son and his twin flame would travel back in time to warn me about my death."

My mouth nearly dropped open. "You knew I'd become the Queen of Pentacles and be able to travel back in time?"

"I knew Ethan's twin flame would be able to travel back in time," he said. "I didn't know her identity—and that she'd also be the Queen of Pentacles—until a few minutes ago when Rosella received a vision that the two of you were here."

I nodded as it all added up. Ethan and I had spent a few minutes in his room preparing to go downstairs. In that time, Rosella's ability would have allowed her to see that we were coming.

"Did he tell you any more than that?" I asked.

"He told me there was no possible future where my death could be stopped. He told me to tell the two of you not to continue trying to save me. There's no outcome except failing, and it will delay you from your true task, which could lead to losing the war against the demons."

I sucked in a sharp breath at the confirmation of what I'd already assumed was true.

Ethan sat completely still, like he refused to believe it.

"Lavinia will use my heart to find the Dark Wand and the Dark Crown," his dad continued, sadly, but firmly. "If she doesn't get my heart, she won't become the Dark Queen of Wands, and the Dark Queen of Pentacles won't rise. Which, as you know, means my death is set in stone."

Ethan's eyes blazed with anger, a burnt orange glow around his irises. "There has to be another way—"

"There is no other way." His dad raised a hand, stopping him from saying any more. "Prince Devyn sees all, and he has confirmed it. I need you to be at peace with the fact that there's nothing you can do to stop this from happening."

The light went out of Ethan's eyes, like this fact had emptied his soul. "When we leave, Time will reject this change," he said. "You'll forget we were ever here."

"Time will only reject the change if the change makes it so the Dark Queens don't rise," his father said. "I came to terms with my death years ago, and will allow my future to play out as fate intended."

"You're not going to do anything?" I asked, shocked.

"Correct."

"Which means the Dark Queens will still rise, and our visit today won't be erased."

"Yes. And whatever we discuss here today will remain in the true timeline."

"We'd remember it anyway," Ethan said. "When we travel, we remember both timelines."

"I know." His father's eyes flashed with sadness. "But now, it will remain in *my* timeline, from now into the Beyond."

Understanding dawned on Ethan's face. "You want this to be goodbye."

"It has to be," his father said, looking relieved when Ethan didn't fight him on it. "Shall we go to my study? There are some things I'd like to share with you, from one king to another."

Ethan nodded, stood up, and followed his dad around the corner, leaving me alone with Rosella.

28

GEMMA

I LOOKED AT THE SEER, unsure what to ask. There was something so ageless about Rosella. It was impossible to explain *what* it was, but somehow, it was like she was all ages at once.

"For you, we haven't met yet," I finally said.

"Yes," she said. "And when we meet in my timeline, you won't know any differently. Everything will happen exactly as you remember."

I nodded, knowing not to question Rosella.

"What's it like?" I asked instead. "To see the future, knowing I can change it so easily?"

She raised an eyebrow. "Has it been easy?"

"Well, no," I admitted. "The future seems pretty stubborn."

She laughed at that. "As you know, I see the most

probable future," she said. "That's the future the present prefers."

"The future I can change."

"You're not the only one who can change the future," she said.

"I know." I sighed. "Mira can, too." I still couldn't get the image of Mira in my bedroom out of my mind, with her Dark Crown and eerily calm dark blue eyes.

"She can," Rosella said. "But that's not what I was referring to."

I tilted my head, confused. "Are you saying there are more time travelers out there?"

"You and your sister are the only time travelers who have ever existed in this Universe," she said. "But the two of you aren't the only two people in the Universe who can change the future."

"I'm confused…"

"I'm talking about *choices*," she said. "Everyone can change the future at any moment—with their decisions. We all have free will. We are all the masters of our own futures."

"True," I said, since while it seemed simple, she wasn't wrong.

"You're going to have many important decisions in the future," she said. "Think each one over carefully. At the same time, trust your instincts. There's a careful balance between emotion and logic. Enter that space—a space of perception and insight—and react and make decisions wisely."

"I'll do my best," I said.

"I know you will."

We sat there for about two hours, and Rosella told me stories of her past. She'd lived for centuries and had crossed the paths of many interesting people in her years—many of them meetings of fate that had resulted in positive change for the future. She'd seen so much in her years, and after it all, she believed in our ability to win against the demons, and in my mission to save Selena and Mira.

Her belief in me helped me believe in myself. Not only *could* I do this, but I *would* do this.

Eventually, Ethan and his dad returned to the living room. Ethan appeared deep in thought, off in his own world, processing everything that was happening.

"It's time," his dad said, and he turned to Ethan and smiled. "I'm proud of you, and I believe in you. Save the Queen of Wands, and save the dragons of Ember."

"I will," Ethan said. "I promise."

His dad nodded. "I'm looking forward to hearing all about it when we meet again in the Beyond. Now, go with Gemma and return to your present in Avalon. The future is waiting for you."

29

GEMMA

ETHAN BARELY SAID a word as we returned to the present and used our keys to travel through the Eternal Library back to Avalon. I wanted to ask him what he and his father had spoken about, but I didn't. Those moments were for him to share when—or *if*—he was ever ready.

When we stepped back into my room, he made no move to return to his.

"I've always cared about you both," he said. "You and Mira. Although I also knew something wasn't right between me and Mira. I was so conflicted and torn. I still am."

I pushed down the resentment attempting to make its way up to my heart. Now—so soon after saying goodbye to his father—wasn't the time for me to release my anger onto him.

Then I remembered what Rosella had told me about reacting from a place of wisdom instead of a place of pure emotion. It was true—my emotions had been getting the best of me recently. They were so strong that I'd pushed them down, forcing myself in a space of pure logic.

Neither of those spaces were positive ones. I needed to find a central space—a balance.

A space of wisdom.

The Crown warmed, as if agreeing with me.

"I was conflicted, too," I admitted, since he deserved the truth. Just because we'd come from a place of lies didn't mean we had to remain in a place of lies. "I hated myself for wishing you'd chosen me. I constantly felt like I was betraying Mira. It was awful."

"I constantly felt like I was betraying her, too," he said. "That day in the cove—the day I met you—I didn't want to leave. I have no idea why I left. There was something special about you. Something that drew me to stay. But I didn't listen to that feeling. I should have. If I'd listened to it, so much would be different right now."

I wanted so badly to tell him that I remembered a time when he *had* stayed.

"I would have loved for you to stay, too," I said instead.

"When I continued along the beach and met Mira,

something told me to go back to the cove," he said. "We *did* go back. But you were gone. From there, Mira was so warm and inviting."

"She's always been the more outgoing twin," I said. "She's easier to get to know."

"Just because someone's easier to get to know doesn't mean they're more worth getting to know," he said. "Not that Mira's not worth getting to know. I truly do care about both of you. But you're the one I love."

"So why not pick me?" I asked. "If you were more drawn to me after meeting both of us, why not choose to be with me instead?"

"I have no idea." He scratched his head, as if genuinely confused. "I guess I didn't want to hurt Mira or cause a rift between the two of you."

I frowned, since it wasn't enough.

I wasn't sure it would ever be enough. He'd had so many chances to be honest with us, but he hadn't done it until forced.

I wished I could understand. I *wanted* to understand.

But I didn't.

"I should have told you," he said.

"Yeah. You should have."

He looked at me with so much longing that I wanted to run into his arms and tell him it would all be okay.

But I couldn't.

Because I wasn't sure it would ever be okay.

"Will you ever be able to forgive me?" he asked.

I thought of Mira saying she hated me, and the anger in her eyes as she'd used her magic against me. I thought about seeing her in my room when she was the Dark Queen of Pentacles—the darkness I'd felt around her, and how when I looked at her, it felt like my twin was gone.

There was no way of knowing if I'd ever get her back.

Ethan should have been strong enough to tell us the truth. The Ethan I'd loved—truly loved with my heart and soul—had stayed with me back in that cove. He'd loved me, and only me. He'd *chosen* me—not because he was forced to, but because it was as natural to him as breathing.

I wanted that to be our reality.

But it wasn't, and it never would be. Not even I—with my ability to travel back in time—could change the choice he'd made.

He sighed in resignation. "I'm going to take your silence as a no."

My heart broke. "I'm sorry," I said. "I wish it wasn't like this."

"Me, too." Sorrow crossed his eyes, and again, I

wished things could be different between us. "Goodnight, Gemma. I hope you sleep well."

With that, he spun around, put his key in the door, and left me alone in my room.

I wanted to go after him.

Once he'd been gone for a few minutes, I put my key into the door and stepped into the ivory hall of the Eternal Library.

Please be here, I thought, and I looked around for Hecate.

The hall was empty.

I cursed and reached for my magic, wanting to throw balls of fire at the marble floor to release my anger. But my magic was blocked, thanks to the spell around Hecate's realm.

Instead, I screamed so loudly that it could have been heard in another dimension. I screamed until my throat hurt and tears streamed down my face. I dug so deep for my magic that it physically hurt—nearly as much as my broken heart.

Once I had nothing more left in me, I laid down and stared up at the details carved in the ivory ceiling.

Would I ever be able to feel whole again? Was I doomed to love someone who only existed in my dreams, but would never be my reality? It felt so wrong, and I hated that there was nothing I could do to make it right.

Could I find it in my heart to forgive him? Would I ever be able to look at him and not be reminded of the fact that my twin flame's decisions had resulted in the loss of my twin sister?

All three of us were broken. And it seemed impossible to become whole again.

Eventually, I forced myself back up. Because while I might feel broken on the inside, there were others who were broken who I could actually help.

Annika and Jacen needed their daughter back.

The *world* needed Selena back.

And I was going to do everything in my power to make it happen.

30

GEMMA

THE NEXT MORNING, Torrence, Reed, Ethan, Skylar, Raven, and I met in Annika and Jacen's quarters. They had a breakfast of mana waiting for us. My mana tasted like one of my favorite breakfasts—French toast and bacon.

Once we were finished, Annika went into her room and came back out with a long, brown cloak.

"Here," she said, handing it to me. "This should keep your identity a secret."

I slipped into the robe and pulled the hood up over my head. "How do I look?" I asked Ethan.

I bit my tongue a second later, realizing that I'd spoken in a friendly way—the way I would have spoken to the Ethan in my dreams.

"Mysterious." He managed a small, teasing smile. "I'd never recognize you."

I tore my gaze away from his, breaking the familiarity between us.

Annika looked back and forth between me and Skylar with tears in her eyes. "I'll never be able to repay the two of you for doing this," she said.

"I'd never ask you to," I said. "The world is at stake. We're doing this for everyone." I glanced at the others. "Are you all ready?"

"Let's do this," Torrence said, and then she took my hands, and Reed took Ethan's hands.

They teleported us to my cove, inside the cave where Mom and Mira had hidden when we'd been attacked by the griffin after getting our magic.

The cave where, in my false memories with Ethan, the two of us had spent time together the day before the ceremony. The cave where I could have sworn he was about to make love to me, despite the dragon tradition that all dragons wait until their first shift, to see if they have a twin flame.

Ethan had been so sure we were twin flames that he was going to defy the tradition of his people.

Torrence flashed out and returned with Skylar, bringing me out of my thoughts and into the present.

"We'll be waiting right here when you get back,"

Torrence said. "Hopefully, we won't have any memories of Selena ever being dead."

"The only people who will remember are me and Skylar," I said, since for everyone else, time would rearrange around them.

"Do you swear you'll tell us everything once you're back?" Ethan asked.

"Yes," I said. "I promise."

He nodded, and I knew that was good enough for him.

"Us, too," Torrence said, referring to her and Reed.

"Are you sure?"

"I helped you save her life," she said. "I want to know about it."

"And are you going to tell her?"

This was a big cause of debate. Annika and Jacen didn't want Selena to know that she and Julian had died in this timeline. They thought it would be easier on her mental health. And I definitely saw their point.

If there was a timeline where I'd died, I wasn't sure how I'd feel or react if someone told me about it.

But Torrence and Reed thought Selena would want to know.

"I know Selena better than anyone else in the world," Torrence said. "I get that her parents are trying to protect her, but she's stronger than they realize."

"Hopefully I'll see that for myself when I finally get to meet her," I said.

"You will."

We nodded to each other, then I turned to Skylar. "You ready?"

"As I'll ever be." She reached forward, and I took her hands in mine.

Take us to the time after Torrence was taken to Circe's island, when Selena decided to follow her there, I thought to the Crown.

We flickered out, and the sun that had been streaming in through the entrance of the cave disappeared. It was nighttime, and voices sounded from outside.

"I have more power than anyone on Avalon," a young, female voice spoke from across the cove. "And we have no idea what Circe wants with Torrence. The longer she's there, the more danger she's in. So I'm going to Circe's island. I can either drop you off at the Vale first, or you can come with me and Reed. But I'm going, and you can't stop me."

Selena.

It had to be.

"What's it gonna be?" a male voice asked—Reed. "Are you coming or not?"

This was it.

The moment Selena made the decision to go with Reed, find the Supreme Mages, and go on her mission to rescue Torrence.

It was the moment I'd come here to change.

"Fine," another male said. He had to be Selena's soulmate, Julian. "If you're going to Circe's island, then I'm coming with you."

I looked to Skylar and nodded.

Her lips were pressed in a thin, determined line. She was ready.

I tiptoed toward the entrance of the cave, stood as close to the wall as possible, and peeked out.

The three of them—Selena, Julian, and Reed—stood in a triangle at the opposite side of the cove. Selena's long, blonde hair blew in the wind, and with the Holy Wand in her hand, she looked like a goddess. Magic radiated from her so intensely that I could feel it, even from this far away.

Her soulmate, Julian, was as perfect looking as a statue carved by one of the great sculptors of the Renaissance. If she was a goddess, he was a god.

They were made for each other. And together, they looked unstoppable.

If only they knew what was coming next.

"Good." Selena turned to Reed. "You've been to Circe's island. Take us there, now."

"I can only take one of you at a time," he said.

"Right," Selena said. "Take me first. Then I'll come back for Julian."

"All right." He reached forward to take her hands.

No.

I ran out of the cave before I realized what I was doing, hurrying until I was nearly halfway across the beach.

"STOP!" I yelled, and they turned to look at me.

Crap.

I was supposed to stay back in the cave. The three of them would surely recognize me, since they'd stopped in the café earlier that day.

As far as they knew, I was a witch with barely any magic.

It needed to stay that way.

I stopped running and pulled the hood further over my head, glad it was dark enough—and that I was still far enough away—that they wouldn't be able to make out my features.

Skylar was the important one. From their point of view, I was the witch who'd been assigned to teleport Skylar to the cove. Insignificant, and not interesting enough to think twice about.

But I couldn't have let Selena take Reed's hands.

If she had, they'd be gone, and I'd have no way to find them again.

I stood perfectly still, hoping that if I didn't move, they'd be too focused on Skylar to pay me any attention.

Skylar ran until she reached them.

Selena dropped her hands back to her sides and tilted her head, confused. "Skylar?" she asked.

"Selena." Skylar paused to catch her breath. "Julian. Reed."

"How do you know Julian's name?" Selena asked. "And how did you know we were here?"

"I'm a prophetess," Skylar reminded them. "And I need to talk to you before you leave for Aeaea."

Selena said nothing.

Instead, she looked over Skylar's shoulder and focused on me. "Come closer," she said. "We won't hurt you."

Reed and Julian turned their attention to me, too.

Panic rushed through me. I couldn't swallow, I couldn't breathe. All I could do was stare at them, frozen, unsure what to say.

There's a way out of this. There has to be.

No solutions came to me.

"She's new to Avalon," Skylar said quickly. "She's powerful, but shy. But she's no matter. Because I had a vision, and I needed to stop you before it was too late."

31

GEMMA

I HELD MY BREATH, praying they didn't ask any more questions.

Selena's focus zipped back to Skylar. So did Reed's and Julian's.

"What type of vision?" Selena asked, and I relaxed, able to breathe again.

"You can't go after Torrence," she said. "You have to go back home. Now."

Magic pulsed through the air, the blue gem on the top of the Holy Wand glowed brighter, and thunder roared overhead.

Selena had caused that thunder. It was her storm magic, gifted to her from the king of the Roman gods, Jupiter.

Incredible.

The blue from the crystal shined on Selena's face, and it was clear that the Queen of Wands was a force to be reckoned with.

We *needed* her to fight with us in the war against the demons.

In that moment, I made a decision.

If Skylar failed, and Selena refused to let Reed go on the rescue mission without her and Julian, I'd interfere and tell Selena everything.

It would be incredibly risky to tell her the truth about my time traveling ability.

There would be a chance that Selena's knowledge of the magic I'd get in the future would create such a big ripple that Time would reject the change.

Telling her would be my last resort. It would go against all of our plans.

But I'd do it anyway. What would I have to lose?

"Torrence is my best friend," Selena said, and the wind picked up enough speed that I had to reach up to keep my hood in place.

Selena's storm magic reminded me of Mira's air magic.

A lump formed in my throat at the thought of my sister.

"I would still be trapped in the Otherworld if it

wasn't for her," Selena continued. "Why's everyone trying to stop me from helping her?"

Right—the last thing her father, Prince Devyn, had done before taking his own life was to try to get her to not go after Torrence.

She hadn't listened to him.

And she'd paid for that decision with her life.

"I'm not stopping you," Reed said. "I'm going to Aeaea, with or without you."

From his determined tone, I knew he meant it. I also knew he meant it because in my present, he'd told me he'd been about to leave for Aeaea that very moment.

It was only Selena's next words that had stopped him from flashing out right then and there.

"I know," she said. "I'm going with you."

"Then who cares what she says?" Reed said, motioning to Skylar. "Let's get out of here."

If Selena so much as moved her hand to reach for Reed's, it would be time to make my move.

Please don't do it, I thought, wishing I could somehow compel Selena to pick up on my energy and listen to it. *I know it's hard, but think with your head and not your heart. The fate of the world depends on it.*

Selena remained focused on Skylar, studying her like she was trying to read her mind. "Tell us what you saw," she said.

I glanced up at the stars and thanked Hecate for listening to my prayers.

"You and Julian can't go with Reed to save Torrence," Skylar said.

"Why not?" Selena asked.

"Because it has to be Reed—and *only* Reed—who goes after her."

"How do you know this?" Selena crossed her arm, looking skeptically at Skylar. "You don't have omniscient sight. You can only see the future as it's going to happen without any interference."

She had a good point. Because none of us had any idea that *only* Reed should go after her. It just seemed like the best way to make sure Selena and Julian stayed alive, and that Reed still ended up in Ember with Torrence.

Because if Reed and Torrence didn't end up in Ember, the Dark Mages might have killed us when we'd arrived. And if they'd killed us...

Time would definitely reject the change.

"Before I got here, you and Julian were going to go with Reed to Aeaea," Skylar said. "I saw what was going to happen if the three of you followed through with that decision." A lie, but close enough. "Every terrible, awful bit of it. You see, to win the war against the demons, each Queen must fight in the final battle. But if you go to Aeaea, you'll die. Avalon will be no more. The people you love most will be gone."

"My parents?" Selena choked up as she forced the words out.

Skylar nodded, saying nothing.

Fear crossed Selena's face.

I held my breath in anticipation. This could be the moment. Right now, Selena could change her mind—and change the future.

"That's only one possible future." Selena sounded like she was grasping for straws. "There has to be another way. Tell me how I'll die. I can change it. I can do something differently once I get to Aeaea."

No, I thought. *The best way to change it is to* not *go to Aeaea.*

One thing was for sure—the Queen of Wands loved her best friend and would do anything to save her. She and Torrence were soul sisters.

I couldn't blame her for wanting to take action to rescue her. I'd do the same for Mira.

Accepting that the best way to help someone you loved was to sit back and let fate run its course was one of the most difficult decisions imaginable.

"If you go to Aeaea, you'll doom us all." Skylar spoke slowly and surely, like prophets did in movies and television shows. "This moment is the turning point. And you need to go home with your soulmate."

"But *why?*"

Wow, Selena was stubborn. Nearly as stubborn as Raven. Annika had fire in her, too. So did I—literally.

I supposed our determination was part of why we were chosen as the Four Holy Queens.

"Because you're the Queen of Wands," Skylar said. "Your duty is to your people. If you turn your back on them and go after Torrence, the war against the demons will be lost. Their power will grow, and Earth will be theirs."

Chills ran up and down my spine at the terrifying reality of our situation.

Please, Selena, I thought. *Listen to her.*

Wasn't this why prophetesses existed? So they could help change the future for the better?

What good were their powers if the people they were trying to help didn't listen to them?

Fire burned inside me, and it took all my willpower not to run across the beach, reveal my identity, and force some sense into Selena.

But Selena hadn't made a decision yet.

I needed to trust Skylar to make this right. So I took a few deep breaths, calmed myself, and grounded my feet in the sand. The earth calmed my fire, wrapping it in trust and confidence.

I was too far away to see the details of Selena's expression, but this was the longest she'd gone without questioning or arguing with Skylar. The wind stilled, as if Selena had stopped throwing her emotions outward, and instead was focusing inward.

It was like she was absorbing and considering what Skylar was telling her.

"So I can't go after Torrence," Selena said slowly, and relief rushed through me. Finally, she was getting it. Hopefully. "But Reed can?"

"Yes," Skylar said. "However, teleporting to Aeaea with no plan or strategy won't be enough. Circe's an immortal sorceress—an extremely powerful one, at that. He'll need backup."

"What kind of backup?" Selena asked.

"He'll need the help of the Supreme Mages."

The final part of the plan.

The Supreme Mages had been there the first time around. We needed to make sure that this reality was as close as possible to the reality I'd come from. Which meant making sure Reed still got the help of the Supreme Mages, so they could get to Aeaea after Torrence destroyed the island and sentence her to imprisonment in Ember. Reed would follow her, and everything in Ember would play out as it had in the original timeline.

At least, that was what we *hoped* would happen. And, given that Torrence was so consumed with dark magic when she landed in Ember that she wasn't affected by the fact that her best friend had just been killed in front of her, she'd likely behave the same way until we got the first half of the Crown, it absorbed her dark magic, and she left Ember.

"How did you know that so quickly?" Selena asked. "Now that we're on a path to a different future, wouldn't you have needed to look into your cards again to see what changed?"

I nearly cursed, since she had a point. But this was also a good thing. Because Selena had said we were on a *path to a different future.*

Which meant Skylar had gotten through to her, and Selena had decided to take another path.

Hopefully, the path where she didn't go after Torrence.

Skylar stilled. "I'm not the only one who has insight into the future," she said. "I've spoken with others, and I'm speaking with you here and *now* for a reason."

It wasn't a lie. It also wasn't the full truth, but hopefully Selena didn't question it further.

"Is she your source?" Selena turned slightly and looked at me.

I froze, and before I had time to think through what to do, Selena started to walk toward me.

But Skylar, with her vampire speed, was faster. She ran toward me in a blur, took my hands, and "Now."

"Wait!" Selena screamed, and a gust of wind blew forward from where she stood.

But my hands were holding Skylar's. So my hood blew back and revealed the Holy Crown that I hadn't placed back in the ether, in case we needed to get out of there quickly.

Take us back to the present, I told the Crown, praying that Selena hadn't gotten a good enough look at me to realize who I was.

Skylar and I flickered out, leaving the dark night behind us and reappearing in the sunlit cove of our present.

32

GEMMA

I BLINKED as my eyes adjusted to the light, and then looked around for Torrence, Reed, and Ethan.

They weren't there.

But only a second was supposed to have passed for them between when Skylar and I had left and now. If they weren't there…

Memories slammed into my mind.

New memories, layering on top of the ones that already existed, until the original ones felt like a dream and the new ones the reality.

"We did it," I said to Skylar, stunned.

She stared out at the ocean, her eyes unfocused as the new memories layered over the old ones in her mind.

"Selena's alive," Skylar said. "But she's not living in Avalon."

"No," I said, and on instinct, I stored the Crown back into the ether. "She's in the Otherworld. Ethan and I met her when we journeyed there to make the ether locker for the Crown. She was ruling by Sorcha's side as Queen of the Half-Bloods."

In my new memories, Selena, Julian, and the freed half-bloods had been fighting the zombies for months. They'd pushed them out of the citadel and the surrounding regions. The citadel had been bright and blooming, and the zombies had never broken through the barrier. There were still zombies in the west, but it was looking like they'd be taken care of soon.

"We never met Gaius, and Genevieve didn't create the ether locker for the Crown for me," I continued. "Selena created it with Julian."

"And your time in Ember?" Skylar asked.

"The same as the first time we were there. As we guessed, since Torrence was dark at that time and her emotions weren't controlling her actions, she didn't act any differently until touching the first half of the Holy Crown. But this time, she didn't return to Avalon to tell Annika and Jacen that their daughter was dead. She went back to reunite with Selena and tell her she was safe."

"The new timeline wrote over the original one." Skylar brought her hands together, her eyes wide. "It actually *worked*."

"It did."

"Now, how are we going to get home?"

"We need to find the nearest door." I reached for my necklace and looked at the stairs winding up the cliff.

The closest door was the one that led inside Twin Pines Café.

"Follow me," I said to Skylar, and I started walking toward the stairs.

"Wait," Skylar said, and I stopped in my path. "What are we going to tell the others?"

It was a good question. Because in the present timeline, the last thing I remembered was having breakfast in Annika's quarters with Annika, Jacen, Raven, Skylar, and Ethan.

After eating, Skylar was going to consult the tarot cards so we could figure out our next move.

Then I'd flickered out, appeared in the cove, and my memories had merged.

"I have no idea," I said. "This is the first time something like this has happened to me."

Skylar frowned, apparently not liking that answer. "They're going to want to know where we went."

I crossed my arms, trying to figure out what we should do.

Torrence didn't want Annika and Jacen to know that Selena had died. So what were we supposed to tell them?

"For what it's worth, I think we should tell them the truth," Skylar said. "But you're the Queen of Pentacles. The decision is yours."

I was still trying to think it through when Torrence, Reed, and Ethan appeared in the cove, at the base of the cliff next to the steps.

"Wow." Torrence glanced at Ethan, who gave her a knowing smirk. "You were right."

I stared at them, startled by their sudden appearance. Especially because given what Torrence had just said, there was only one conclusion I could draw...

"You knew we were here," I said to Ethan, and he nodded. "How?"

It didn't make sense.

In their reality, we hadn't needed to go back in time to save Selena, since Selena had never died. The entire mission we'd just successfully completed didn't exist. Which meant the group of us had never gone to the cove. They hadn't been waiting for us when we'd returned from the past because they hadn't needed to come here in the first place.

"We were having breakfast with Annika, Jacen, Raven, and Skylar, and then the two of you flickered out." He glanced at Skylar, then back to me. "Annika, Jacen, and Raven continued talking, as if nothing strange had happened. When I asked where you were, they were dazed and said they didn't know. It was like the confusion people have when we use or talk about our keys in front of them."

"But *you* realized what had happened," I said.

"I did. And a second later, the memories of the original timeline flooded my mind. I remembered the mission to save Selena, and I knew that in the original timeline, Torrence, Reed, and I had dropped you and Skylar off at the cove."

"That sounds confusing."

"It was," he said. "I asked Annika to bring me to Torrence and Reed, because I thought maybe they remembered both timelines, too. But when I asked them if their memories came back, they looked at me like I was crazy."

"We still think you're crazy," Torrence said.

"There was no time to tell them everything that had happened." Ethan shrugged. "I just told them that you and Skylar were at the cove, that I needed them to teleport me here, and that I'd explain everything once we got here."

"And now we're here," Torrence said. "So—explain."

I thought back to what she already knew. Because in the original timeline, Torrence and Reed only knew that I was the Queen of Pentacles and could travel back in time because we needed their help for the mission to save Selena.

In the new timeline where Selena was alive, we hadn't had to go to Torrence and Reed, since we hadn't needed to save Selena. The last time I'd seen the two of them had been when we'd parted ways in Ember. Back then, we'd only had the first half of the Crown, and had no idea who was going to be the fourth Queen.

Which meant we had a *lot* to catch them up on.

"Skylar and I just got back from saving Selena," I started, figuring it was best to drop it on them all at once. "You see, where I come from, Selena was killed by the Supreme Mages during her attempt to rescue you from Aeaea."

Reed's expression hardened. "Selena never came with me to rescue Torrence," he said. "She was going to, but then Skylar and a witch from Avalon teleported here and warned her not to go. They said if she did, she'd die..." He studied me, and realization dawned in his eyes. "You," he said. "*You* were the witch who brought Skylar to the cove. You were wearing the same robe you have on now."

"Yes." I smiled at how quickly he was catching on. "I needed the hood to hide my identity. Hopefully Selena didn't see me when it blew off in that last second."

"She did see you," Reed said. "She went to check on you in the café. You and Mira were working at the counter, so she figured she'd been mistaken."

"She wasn't mistaken," I said. "I was at the café. I was also here with Skylar while she delivered the message to you and Selena. Like I said, we just returned from that mission. We've been back for about ten minutes."

I stood there patiently, waiting for them to put the pieces together.

"No. Freaking. Way," Torrence finally said, and she turned to Ethan. "You said before that you remembered different timelines. Are you trying to say that…" Her eyes widened, and she refocused on me. "Did you come here that day from the future?"

"I did." I pulled the Holy Crown out of the ether and placed it on my head. "I'm the Queen of Pentacles. And the Holy Crown gifted me with the ability to travel through time."

The Torrence from the original timeline got her wish—the version of her in this timeline learned the details of Selena's original fate.

"Wow," Reed said once we'd finished explaining. "This is heavy."

Ethan raised an eyebrow. "Did you just quote *Back to the Future?*"

"You bet I did."

I looked back and forth between the two of them and smiled, having a feeling that this was going to be the start of a beautiful friendship.

"I'm going to tell Selena," Torrence decided. "She'd want to know that her decision not to go after me was the right one to make."

"And Annika?" I asked.

"I'll leave that decision to Selena."

I nodded, since that seemed like the best way to go.

"So," Ethan said. "We succeeded in our mission to save Selena. What's next?"

"We find Mira," I said. "We'll bring her to Avalon, and I'll take some of the darkness from her, like I did for Torrence."

"How *did* you do that?" Torrence asked.

"I'm not sure. But once we get Mira to Avalon, I'll figure it out."

If she got accepted to Avalon.

Now that she was dark, who was to say she wouldn't be turned away?

I shook the thought away, since it didn't matter. If Mira wasn't accepted in Avalon, I'd bring her somewhere else. The Haven or the Vale.

But what if she traveled back in time while there? We'd be right back to where we started.

The Eternal Library, I realized. *She won't be able to use her dragon magic in the Library.*

I'd tell Ethan the idea later. Together, we'd figure it out.

"I guess now we go back to Avalon," Torrence said. "And from there, I'll head to the Otherworld to find Selena."

33

GEMMA

I wasn't ready to announce to all of Avalon that I was the Queen of Pentacles, but Annika still gave me a tour of the island, which took up the rest of the day. She was bright, optimistic, and happy—an entirely different person than I'd met in the original timeline.

The island was incredible, and the tour included riding a unicorn across a lake and flying on the back of a wyvern. I could see why Raven thought none of the kingdoms on Earth compared to Avalon.

Avalon was a true, utopian paradise.

But as beautiful as the island was, it could never be my home. Not without my mom—and potentially Mira—there with me.

The entire time I was on the tour, I kept thinking about Ethan. Mainly, how did he remember both timelines, even though he hadn't come with me on the trip to save Selena? The timeline should have morphed around him and erased the original one, like it had for Torrence and Reed. The only ones who should have remembered both timelines were me and Skylar.

Why was it different for Ethan?

Which brought me back to the question that had consumed me since I'd been poisoned with that nightshade—was what I'd experienced with Ethan while I'd been unconscious a dream or an alternate reality, like what I'd theorized with Rosella?

The experience with the nightshade was going to haunt me until I had answers. The emotional agony it had been causing me was unbearable. I'd pushed it down since Mira had turned dark, but now that we didn't have an immediate mission we were trying to complete, the pain had returned at full force.

It was time for me to do something about it.

So that night, I waited for everyone to go to sleep. Then I used my key and entered the Eternal Library.

Hecate stood in the center of the ivory hall, waiting for me. Her gown was as dark as night, and the crescent moon on her forehead glowed as she locked eyes with mine.

"Well done," she said simply.

I almost asked if she was talking about how Skylar and I had saved Selena, but I stopped myself.

Because that wasn't the question I'd come here to ask.

"We needed all four Holy Queens alive to defeat the demons," I said instead.

"Like I said—well done."

That confirmed it.

She knew I'd changed the timeline.

"Shall we?" She motioned toward the doors that led to the room with the endless bookshelves, and I followed her inside.

What more does she know? I wondered as she walked to stand in front of the podium. *Does she know what I'm going to ask before I come here to ask it? What are the limits to the knowledge that can be found in the Library's shelves? Are there any limits?*

So many questions.

But I could only ask one.

"What's the truth behind the visions I had when I'd been poisoned by the nightshade?" I asked.

"I've been waiting for you to be ready to come to me with this question," she said, and then she released the starry smoke from her eyes, its tendrils perusing the shelves.

It returned with a thin, blood-red book. The pages flew open, landing on one near the center.

She glanced at it, then stepped aside, making room in front of the podium. "You need to see this one for yourself," she said.

I inhaled sharply. "I'm allowed to touch the books?"

"I decide what's best seen and what's best told. And the answer to this question is one I feel you need to see."

I walked forward, stood in front of the podium, and looked down at the book. The letters swirled together before I could make out the words, rotating in a hypnotizing vortex that tugged at my skin and pulled me inside until I was falling and spinning like Alice tumbling down the hole to Wonderland.

The world pieced itself back together, and I found myself standing in the living room of the cabin that made up the Seventh Kingdom—the same place I'd been standing when Ethan had first placed the Holy Crown on my head.

This time, the room was empty. It was also brighter than before, thanks to the rays of sunlight streaming in through the windows.

I looked down at my hands—they were pale and transparent, like how they got after drinking invisibility potion. My entire body was invisible. When I walked forward to touch the back of one of the chairs, my hand went right through it. And my footsteps didn't make a sound.

I was more than just invisible. I was a true observer, unable to create any changes in the environment around me.

Suddenly, someone gasped from behind the door that led to the bedroom. It was the room I'd landed in when I'd first time traveled and watched Ethan place the Crown on my head.

Muffled voices sounded from the other side.

I walked toward the door and reached for the knob, but my hand went through it.

I narrowed my eyes at it in frustration. But there was nothing to be frustrated about. Because I wasn't corporeal. So I simply stepped forward and walked through the door, as if it wasn't there. I didn't feel a thing.

Inside the bedroom, Constance was sitting straight up in her bed, her eyes wide.

Katherine, Genevieve, and Isemay were slowly waking up and rubbing their eyes, as if they'd been asleep for years.

No—not years.

Centuries.

This was the moment the four of them woke from the sleeping spell that froze them in time.

Katherine blinked a few times, then focused on Constance. "What's today's date?" she asked.

Constance answered with a date I recognized immediately—the day before my birthday.

Mira and I would be receiving our magic the next day.

But our birthday had been months ago. When we'd arrived in the Seventh Kingdom, Katherine had told us that they'd awoken from the spell that morning, so they'd be there to give us the second half of the Crown.

Assuming the book was showing me the truth, then Katherine had lied.

But *why* would she lie? What did it have to do with the nightshade induced hallucinations I'd had of Ethan?

Katherine studied Constance, who was stunned speechless. "What did you see?" she asked.

"Something horrible," Constance said slowly, like she was still trapped in the haze of her vision.

"Don't leave us in suspense or anything," Genevieve said snidely.

Katherine glared at her. "Mind your manners," she said, and Genevieve huffed and rolled her eyes. Then she refocused on Constance. "Do you need blood?"

"No," Constance replied. "I'm still full from our final meal before we went to sleep."

They all nodded, as if they felt the same.

"Did your vision have to do with the Queen of Pentacles?" Katherine asked.

"It does."

"What about her?"

Constance met the queen's gaze, fear shining in her eyes. "Tomorrow, the twins will receive their dragon magic," she said. "And soon afterward, one of them will die."

34

GEMMA

QUEEN KATHERINE WAS out of bed in a second. "One of those twins is destined to become the Queen of Pentacles," she said. "Is the twin that dies the one who's meant to become the Queen?"

"I don't know," Constance said. "At this point, either one of them may become the Queen."

"Then neither of them can die before that happens."

Genevieve swung her legs over the side of the bed, slow to stand up. "They can," she said. "And according to Constance's vision, one of them will."

"I understand that," Katherine snapped. "But we're guarding the second half of the Crown because we're waiting for the Queen of Pentacles to journey here and find it. She can't do that if she's dead." She faced Isemay, who was the groggiest of them all. "You're the one who spoke with Prince Devyn. He told you to tell us to wait for the twins here. *Both* of them."

"He did," Isemay said.

"Are you sure something didn't get lost in translation?"

"I'm sure."

"Then it looks like we're going to have to go to the Otherworld and speak with him ourselves," Genevieve said. "He'll know which twin is destined to become Queen."

"I'm afraid that won't be possible," Constance said. "Because Prince Devyn is dead."

The three of them silenced.

"How?" Genevieve finally asked. "He's immortal, and he has omniscient sight. He can see every possible way anyone could ever try to kill him, and then he can stop it from happening."

"He chose to end his own life," Constance said solemnly.

Silence again.

"How do you know this?" Genevieve asked. "You're a prophetess. You can see the future—not the past."

"I saw it while sleeping."

"We didn't dream while sleeping under the spell."

"We didn't," Constance agreed. "But I had visions. And the vision I had right now was strong enough to wake me, and therefore the three of you, from the spell."

I watched and listened, as confused as Queen Katherine. Because clearly neither Mira nor I had died.

Constance's vision had been wrong.

Then I thought back to the conversation I'd had with Rosella back at Ethan's house.

When prophetesses get visions, it's an opportunity for them to change the future.

They must have saved whichever one of us was supposed to die the next day.

But how? And what did this have to do with my dreams of Ethan while I'd been unconscious because of the nightshade?

"Isemay—go fetch some snow from outside, bring it in, and melt it," Queen Katherine said. "I think we should have something to sip on while Constance tells us the details of her vision."

They gathered around the kitchen table a few minutes later, each with a glass of water in front of them.

Unable to sit, I stood next to the table, anxious for Constance to continue.

"I saw the night the twins will get their elemental

magic," she started. "Tomorrow night. The blonde twin—Mira—will be gifted with magic over water and air. The brunette—Gemma—will be gifted with earth and fire."

"So they're equally as powerful," Katherine said. "Both of them strong enough to potentially become Queen."

"They have an equal amount of magic inside of them," Constance said. "But one twin is naturally more in tune with her magic and will be more confident using it."

"Which one?"

"Gemma."

"Fire and earth."

Constance nodded.

"Is she the one who dies?" Katherine asked.

"No."

I gasped, although of course, none of them heard me.

Mira had been fine that night. She'd used as much magic as she could, and then Ethan had brought her to the cave with Mom, where they'd been safe until Ethan and I had killed the griffin.

Katherine sat straighter, determination shining in her eyes. "Tell me everything."

Constance started from the moment around the bonfire when Mira and I had been gifted with our magic. She told them about the griffin's attack—how it had swooped down and grabbed our cousin, and how I'd tried and failed to direct Mira on how to use her power over air to try to save her.

No—*I* hadn't failed.

Mira simply hadn't been practiced enough with her magic to know what to do. And who could blame her? We'd gotten our magic *minutes* before all of that had happened.

Constance continued on to tell the others about how the griffin had killed Rebecca, too.

"The twins were losing against the griffin," she said. "I don't think either of them would have survived if Gemma's boyfriend, Ethan, hadn't rushed in from the sidelines to help."

Gemma's boyfriend.

The two words echoed in my mind.

Because Ethan wasn't my boyfriend.

Well, I had no idea what to call him *now*. But on the night we'd gotten our magic, he most definitely hadn't been my boyfriend.

Constance's vision had to be wrong. Because on the day before we'd gotten our magic, Ethan had been *Mira's* boyfriend.

There was nothing the foursome sitting at the table

right now could have done after this point to change that.

"Ethan's a powerful dragon prince gifted with magic over fire and air," Constance continued. "He'll try to bring the twins to safety in a nearby cave so he can fight the griffin alone."

"Let me guess," Genevieve said. "The strong twin—Gemma—isn't going to want to sit back in a cave while her boyfriend faces this monster?"

"Ethan wasn't my boyfriend," I said, although of course, none of them heard me.

"Sort of," Constance said. "Kelly's mother—Sasha—will be in shock, unable to move away from her daughter's body. She's a sitting duck for the griffin. Gemma will refuse to leave her there. She'll tell Ethan to bring Mira to the cave while she gets Sasha. The griffin will still be far out in the ocean at this point—where it dropped Rebecca to her death—so Ethan will have time to bring Mira to safety. But he'll follow Gemma, leaving Mira stranded on the beach. He and Gemma will get into a fight as they try to save Sasha. During this time, the griffin will zoom toward Mira, snatch her up, and kill her."

No.

That wasn't what had happened.

I'd gone to Sasha alone.

She'd rejected my help.

So I'd spun around, faced the griffin, and threw as much fire at it as possible. Then, after getting Mira safely to the cave, Ethan had joined me and helped me fight.

But if what Constance was saying was true, then Ethan and I had gotten into some sort of argument about how to help Sasha.

I hadn't turned around and thrown those initial blazes of fire at the griffin. I hadn't slowed the griffin down.

And then Mira—who hadn't been in the cave, because Ethan had followed me instead of taking her—had been standing on the beach, perfect bait for the griffin.

Except none of this had happened.

So why was the book from the Eternal Library showing this to me? Was it another imaginary world, like the one I'd experienced with Ethan after being poisoned by the nightshade?

No, I realized. *This is the world from my hallucination. It's what would have happened there the next night.*

I'd woken up from the "alternate world" the night before Mira and I had gotten our magic. I'd been spending time with Ethan in the cave, mentally preparing for the ceremony.

In the alternate world, this is what would have happened during the ceremony.

In that world, Mira would have died.

If I'd been Ethan's girlfriend instead of Mira, he would have followed me when I'd gone to help Sasha, instead of taking Mira to the cave.

In the alternate world, Ethan's love for me had gotten my twin killed.

"Gemma's magic is strong," Constance continued. "After Mira's death, she'll launch blasts of fire at the griffin and char it to the bones. She's fully capable of killing the griffin alone."

"So you think Ethan should have brought Mira to that cave and left Gemma to handle the situation on her own," Isemay said.

"Since I can only see the future as it will play out at this moment without interference, I can't say what will happen if he takes Mira to that cave and lets Gemma take care of the griffin," Constance said. "I *can* tell you that if Mira's in that cave, she won't be sitting there as easy bait."

But I hadn't fought the griffin on my own. I'd only shot the first blasts. Then Ethan had joined me, and we'd killed the griffin *together*.

Still... I'd shot those first blasts. And those were

strong blasts. I'd weakened the griffin and slowed its progress significantly.

Ethan had definitely helped. But maybe I hadn't been giving myself enough credit for what I'd done that night.

Genevieve sighed and leaned back in her chair. "It's wonderful to think about what would have happened if Ethan had prioritized Mira's life, especially since it sounds like Mira could have used the extra protection," she said. "But how, exactly, do we get him to leave his girlfriend out in the open like that?"

"I have an idea," Katherine said, and then the world blurred around me like the letters had blurred on the page of the book, and I fell back down the pit before she could say any more.

35

GEMMA

I REAPPEARED in the cave at the cove, in the same ghost-like form. A dozen candles were lit inside, and Ethan and I sat next to each other. He was talking to me with a flame in each hand, and then he snuffed them out.

I knew this moment.

It was my last memory of the alternate world I'd shared with Ethan. It was the moment he'd told me about twin flames.

We looked at each other with love shining in our eyes, as if it was taking all of our self-control not to fall back into each other's arms.

"But I'm not a dragon," the other version of myself—the one from my alternate memories—said. Even though I was only an onlooker right now, I remembered what it was like to be sitting where she was sitting, my arm brushing against Ethan's as I looked into his soulful hazel eyes. "So I can't have a twin flame."

"You'll have dragon magic," Ethan said. "That's what connects twin flames—our magic. Every twin shares at least one element with the other."

"I get my magic tomorrow."

"Yes." He watched me carefully.

I watched the other version of me carefully, too, since what she was about to say were the last words I remembered before I'd been pulled out of the dream.

"Do you think there's a chance—"

She stopped speaking, and her gaze snapped to where I was standing.

I froze.

Was she *seeing* me?

I wracked my mind for an explanation about why I was there, but came up blank. How could I explain what I didn't understand?

Then I heard footsteps behind me.

Someone else was there.

The other version of me wasn't looking at me. She was looking at whoever was walking inside the cave.

I turned around… and there was Katherine, dressed in the same animal hide winter gear she'd worn when she'd met with us in Antarctica. She was ridiculously out of place in the beach in Australia, yet she walked with her head held high—with the confidence of a queen. With her blonde hair that was so pale it was nearly white, she looked like some sort of angel.

"Gemma." Her voice was calm and steady. "Ethan."

They stood.

"Who are you?" he asked.

"I'm someone you're going to meet in the future," she said mysteriously.

"So you're a prophetess." He inhaled deeply. "A gifted vampire."

My other self watched her, mesmerized, clutching onto Ethan's hand. Queen Katherine was the first vampire she'd ever met. She was the first *supernatural* she'd ever met, excluding Ethan.

And excluding Selena, Torrence, Reed, and Julian, given that they'd wiped her—our?—memory of meeting them.

Queen Katherine walked closer and stopped a few meters away from Ethan and the other me. "You're correct that I'm a gifted vampire," she said. "I'm not, however, a prophetess."

"Then what's your gift?" Ethan asked.

"Superior compulsion."

The other me stood strong, and if she was scared, I couldn't tell. "What does that mean?"

"It means that I want the two of you to forget everything that's happened since you met," Katherine said, the melodic sound of the compulsion in her voice hypnotizing as she spoke.

Ethan and other-Gemma's eyes went blank.

Horror sliced through me like shards of glass through my soul.

"No," I said, although of course, none of them heard.

"On that first day in the cove, you didn't tell Ethan your secret," Katherine said to the other me. Then she turned her focus to Ethan. "You got up and continued walking along the beach, where you came across Mira surfing with her friends. You spent time with Mira that day—not with Gemma. Mira's the twin you chose to be with, and the twin you fell in love with. You and Gemma barely know each other. She's only in your life because she's Mira's sister."

She continued on, weaving a tale of Ethan and Mira's relationship. It was a tale I knew well, since Mira had always loved telling me about what she and Ethan did together and how close they were with each other. It was the story I remembered living—it was what had happened in my real world.

As Katherine spoke, the universe shifted around me,

like puzzle pieces being pulled apart and forced back into places they didn't quite fit.

"Now, both of you will return home and forget that all of this happened," she said with finality in her tone. "Life will be as I said, and no one will question that it was ever any different."

The jagged ends of the puzzle pieces that made up this new reality smoothed over and locked into place.

My stomach swirled, and I wrapped my arms around it, feeling like I was about to be sick.

This can't be happening.

And yet, it was.

Ethan and other-Gemma's eyes refocused, although they still looked dazed, like they weren't fully present. Saying nothing, they walked out of the cave, not acknowledging Queen Katherine, and not acknowledging each other. It was like they didn't even see each other there.

They turned the corner out of the entrance, and Queen Katherine exhaled, a final whoosh of energy escaping her lips. Then she collapsed and passed out on the sandy ground.

Superior compulsion, I thought as the world swirled around me for the third time that day. *The ability to change the memories of not just the people she was talking to, but of everyone they were connected to as well.*

The ability to change reality as we knew it.

That was my last thought before I was pulled into the pit and fell through, until I landed back where I'd been standing in front of the open book in Hecate's Eternal Library.

36

GEMMA

I SLAMMED THE BOOK SHUT, stormed past Hecate, and hurried through the ivory hall. Fire fueled my blood even though my dragon magic was blocked in Hecate's realm.

This can't be happening.

Except it was. And it made my feelings for Ethan that I'd been fighting for months make a crazy amount of sense.

I used my key to leave the Library, and stepped into Mary's bedroom in the Haven. It was daytime there, so she was sleeping, as expected.

She woke at the sound of the door shutting behind me.

"Gemma?" She yawned, then sat up in bed, instantly alert. "What's going on?"

"I need to speak to Queen Katherine," I said. *"Now."*

I would have barged into Katherine's room if I knew where in the Haven she was staying. There were so many guest rooms that it would be a waste of time to bang on the doors of each one.

Plus, as the Queen of Pentacles, I could do as I pleased. Including barging into the leader of the Haven's room during the height of day and waking her up when I needed help.

"Of course." Mary got out of bed and ran her fingers through her long hair. "Follow me."

She walked me down the path to the guest hotel, glancing at me hesitantly. The only other people awake at this hour were the tiger shifters, who stood on guard in their human forms. They watched me and Mary as we walked, but remained silent, as guards were supposed to do.

The ground rumbled beneath my feet with every step I took.

"Do you care to share what this is about?" Mary asked as we neared the hotel.

"No."

She nodded, as if she'd expected that answer.

We silently entered the hotel lobby, walked into the elevator, and she pressed the button for the fifth floor.

She led me all the way down the hall, to the last room on the left.

"This is it," she said, and I flung the door open with so much force that it slammed against the wall.

Katherine stirred in her bed.

The bed frame was made of wood.

I reached for my earth magic and used it to raise the bed nearly to the ceiling, shaking it and dumping Katherine onto the floor. Then I let the bed fall back down next to her with a loud thump, satisfied when she flinched.

"Leave us," I said to Mary.

She left the room and closed the door behind her, shock splattered across her face.

I reached for my witch magic and chanted the Latin for a sound-blocking spell. The magic surged forth from me—more witch magic than I'd ever harnessed before. The walls glowed fiery orange, then dimmed out.

The spell had worked.

No one outside of the room would be able to hear the conversation I was about to have with Katherine.

"Get up," I said to her, and she did as I commanded.

Her pale blonde hair was mussed from sleep, but her expression was as royal and confident as ever.

She knows that I know.

What *else* would I be so raging mad about?

But she just stood there, staring at me with her calm, vampiric gaze. She was waiting for me to speak first.

"You saved Mira's life back in the cove," I started, since that was the one good thing that had come from what she'd done. "Now, reverse the compulsion. Give everyone their memories back. Their memories of the *true* past."

My words hung heavily in the air.

If she was surprised, she didn't show it.

"How did you find out?" she asked.

"I'm the Queen of Pentacles." I didn't want to get into the details of it, because the details didn't matter. "And I'm *commanding* you to fix this."

"I saved your sister's life," she said. "You should be grateful."

"I *am* grateful for that," I said. "Eternally so. But the task is done. Now, give them their real memories back."

"I'm afraid I can't do that."

"You're gifted with superior compulsion," I said. "Of course you can do it."

"My magic has limits," she said. "One of them is that I can't undo anything I've done."

"Why not?"

"I have no idea. But perhaps it's similar to the reason why you can't travel back to the same time in the past more than once."

"What reason is that?"

"I can only guess," she said. "But I've always felt like it was because the mind can only handle so many changes to its perceived reality before going into overdrive."

"You're lying." I couldn't imagine what reason she could have for wanting to keep their memories as they were, but I'd figure it out one way or the other.

"I'm not lying," she said. "I'll drink truth potion and tell you again, if it will help you believe me."

She was bluffing.

She *had* to be bluffing.

"All right." I walked over to the nightstand, picked up the pen, and wrote on the pad of paper.

Send a vial of truth potion to room 535.

I folded it up and sent it as a fire message to the apothecary. There were always witches working in the apothecary—even when the rest of the kingdom was asleep.

I reached for my fire magic and faced Katherine, half-expecting her to run.

She stayed where she was.

"I'm truly sorry for how this affected you and Ethan," she said. "But he's your twin flame. Deep down, he knows he loves you—that's why he crowned you as Queen. I might have erased your past, but the two of you still have a future."

"If what you're saying is true, he'll never remember *falling* in love with me," I said, the truth of it hurting my heart. "And what about Mira? You saved her life, but you broke her soul."

"Would you have preferred it if I did nothing?"

"I would have preferred it if you hadn't played with our emotions by changing our entire perception of the past."

"It was the clearest path to making sure both of you lived," she said. "And it worked. If there was another way, why wouldn't you have already gone back in time to change it instead of coming to me and asking me to reverse it?"

"That's exactly what I'm going to do," I said. "After making sure you're telling the truth about not being able to reverse your compulsion."

"What reason would I have to lie?"

I said nothing, since I was wondering the same thing.

Finally, there was a knock on the door. I opened it and found a young witch standing there with a vial of light blue truth potion.

"Thanks." I took the potion and closed the door before she could ask any questions. Then I marched across the room and shoved the vial in Katherine's face. "Here," I said. "Drink."

She took the vial from me, uncapped it, and I braced

myself for her to dump the contents onto the floor. Instead, she raised it to her lips and drank it down.

Her pupils dilated as it kicked in.

"Happy?" she asked.

"Yes."

For the next hour, the potion would force her to answer any question with the truth.

"Can you reverse your compulsion?" I kept the question as simple as possible.

"No," she said without hesitation.

She didn't even try to fight it.

She was telling the truth.

Every piece of hope I'd been holding on to since closing that book in the Library shattered.

But I had one more option. The chance of it working was slim to none, but it was still an option.

I needed to travel back to the past. I needed to stop Katherine before she compelled me and Ethan in that cave, and I needed to convince her to find another way.

If she could pull it off, we'd have our memories back.

If she couldn't, and if Mira died that night in the cove, then Time would reject the change and the true past would be lost forever.

37

GEMMA

I used my key to leave Katherine's room, and I stepped back in the Library. Hecate wasn't there, since I'd already used my question for the day.

I spun around, put my key back into the lock, and walked into the main room of the cabin in Antarctica. Everything was how we'd left it—including the dent in the wood where Mira had thrown me into the wall.

Fire raged inside me at the sight of it.

But this time, it wasn't anger at Ethan for lying to us and causing a permanent rift between me and my twin. Because Ethan had to have been just as confused and beaten up about his feelings as I'd been.

It was anger at the true person responsible for what had happened—Katherine.

I closed my eyes and thought to the Crown, *Take me*

back to when Constance had her vision of what was originally supposed to have happened on the night Mira and I got our magic.

Nothing happened.

I pushed harder.

Still, nothing.

I cursed and used my magic to raise a wooden chair from the floor and throw it against the wall. The chair splintered into pieces.

Why can't I go back to that moment?

I hadn't been there before.

Except... I had. Not in my actual form, but in ghost form. Or whatever form it was technically called when the book from the Eternal Library had let me invisibly observe what had happened here all those months ago.

Time for a new method.

Take me back to when the four of them were in this room and Katherine said she had an idea.

It was the moment after my ghost form had been pulled out of the scene.

I flickered out and reappeared in the same spot, at the moment I'd requested.

This time, all four of them turned their heads to stare at me.

"Gemma?" Constance was the first to speak.

Of course she was—she was the only one who knew what I looked like, since she'd seen me in her vision.

"Hi." I shuffled my feet awkwardly and gave her a small smile.

Where was I supposed to begin with my explanation of everything? There were so many timelines—and now an *imaginary* timeline created by Katherine's compulsion—that it was getting hard to keep track.

Isemay stared at my head like an alien was sitting on top of it. "That's the Holy Crown," she said, and then she hurried into the bedroom—the same place where Genevieve had gone to fetch their half of the Crown when they'd presented it to us. She returned with the frosted box, placed it on the table, and opened it.

Their half of the Crown was inside—exactly where it was supposed to be.

"Impossible." Genevieve's eyes widened at the sight of the half of the Crown in the box. Then she looked to me in confusion. "Why are you wearing a fake Holy Crown?"

"This isn't a fake Holy Crown," I said. "It's the real deal."

"It can't be."

"It is."

"So you're claiming to be the Queen of Pentacles," Katherine said coldly, clearly not believing it.

"I *am* the Queen of Pentacles. And I'm here to give you a warning."

"No," Constance said, and we all looked to her. "This doesn't make sense. I just saw you and your twin in a vision. Neither of you have your dragon magic yet. What little witch magic you have is untrained and useless."

"Apparently not," Isemay said. "Since she just teleported here."

Genevieve sniffed in my general direction. "I don't smell enough witch magic on her for her to be able to do something as advanced as teleportation."

"You're right—I didn't teleport here," I said. "I time traveled."

They all silenced.

I didn't think I'd ever stop feeling the thrill of dropping the time travel bomb on people for the first time.

"I'm here from the future," I started before any of them could get a word in. "I know you just had a vision—one where you saw my twin sister get attacked and killed by a griffin at the ceremony tomorrow night where we'll receive our dragon magic," I said to Constance. Then, I turned my attention to Katherine. "To change that future, you're going to use your gift of superior compulsion to make us all believe that Mira's

Ethan's girlfriend, so he'll bring her to safety instead of going after me."

"I haven't even voiced that idea yet," Katherine said. "How do you know all of this?"

"I already told you. I'm from the future. I know all of this because I've already lived through it."

I watched her expression change as acceptance sank in.

Well, not *acceptance.* Not quite yet. But realization that what I was saying might be possible.

"I'm listening," she said.

They hadn't asked me to sit, but I pulled out one of the empty chairs—the one I'd just destroyed in my present—and joined them at the table.

"Your idea goes as planned," I said to Katherine. "After compelling us all to believe that Ethan's dating Mira instead of me, he gets her to the cave safely, and all three of us survive the griffin attack. We learn how to use our magic and eventually make our way here with the first half of the Crown, where I become the Queen of Pentacles and receive the gift of power over the fifth element. Time travel."

"Very interesting." Katherine nodded, as if I hadn't just changed her entire perception of reality as she knew it. "So, if what I'll do is a success, then why are you here?"

"I'm here because Ethan's my twin flame, and you *erased* the months we spent together when we fell in love," I said, venom dripping from my tone. "My twin sister hates me because she thinks Ethan and I betrayed her, even though the relationship she believes she had with him is a lie. So I'm here to beg you to figure out another way to save my sister. A way that doesn't result in such a giant, agonizing, heartbreaking mess."

38

GEMMA

After speaking with Queen Katherine, I said goodbye to the four of them and returned to the present.

The wall was still dented.

The chair was still splintered.

Whatever change Katherine had attempted—*if* she'd attempted one at all—hadn't worked.

Fire rose inside me, swirling around and pleading to be let loose so it could eat the cabin alive. It consumed me, building up until it burst forth in an explosion of orange light, so bright that I wondered if it was visible from space.

Flames surrounded me, heatwaves pulsing all around like I was inside a convection oven. The fire crackled and popped as it ate the wood, the burning remains filling my senses.

Once I'd released more fire than I thought was possible to have inside me, it died down, and I gazed around.

The cabin was ashes at my feet.

The snow on the island had melted, and I was standing on soft, squishy mud.

Panic filled me, and I stood there, shellshocked as I stared at the smooth ocean and snow-covered mountains.

Because there was no door. Without a door, I couldn't use my key to get to Avalon. I was stranded on an island in the middle of Antarctica. I didn't even have a pen and paper to send a fire message to ask Genevieve for help, since she was the only witch in the world who'd been to this island, and therefore, the only witch who'd be able to teleport here to rescue me.

But as quickly as the panic had set in, so did the solution.

I needed to think fourth dimensionally.

Take me back to eight hours ago, I told the Crown, since that was a safe enough time when I wouldn't run into my past self in the Library when I'd asked Hecate about my memories with Ethan.

I flickered out, and in what seemed like a split-second, the cabin reformed around me. It was as good as new, minus the dent in the wall. The only difference from when I was there five minutes ago was that the sun's rays were streaming in through the windows on the opposite side of the room.

Unless I needed to return here in the past, this was the last time I'd see the Seventh Kingdom.

I used my key to enter my room in the Haven. From there, I traveled back to the present, then returned to my room in Avalon. It had only been an hour since I'd left, and everyone in the kingdom was fast asleep.

After my adventures, I was exhausted. But I couldn't go to bed yet.

Not before talking to Ethan.

I changed into my pajamas, then used the key to walk into Ethan's room.

He was awake, reading a book in bed. The moment I entered, he smiled and put the book down. "Everything okay?" he asked.

No.

"I just got back from the Library," I said instead.

"Is Hecate still there?" he asked, apparently figuring out from my tone that I'd spoken with her. "I haven't used my question for the day."

"She's not there anymore." I took a deep breath, then sat on the edge of the bed, leaving not much space between us.

He studied me, like he was trying to see into my soul. "What happened?"

Where could I possibly begin?

I had no idea.

So I leaned forward and kissed him.

He kissed me back hungrily, like he was dying of thirst and I was the liquid he needed to survive.

Love surged through my soul, and time disappeared around me. I wanted this moment to last forever.

His kisses slowed, and he pulled back, cupping my cheek with his hand and looking down at me with the familiarity I remembered from when we'd kissed back in Lilith's lair.

"This has happened before," he said slowly. "Not just that one other time. *Lots* of other times."

Hope rose inside me, and I nodded. "What do you remember?"

"You and me, in your room," he started. "And then in the cave…" He trailed off, and his gaze went blank, like he'd lost his train of thought.

"Yes." My heart beat faster, like it was going to explode with anticipation. "In the cave, the day before I received my magic, when you told me you thought we were twin flames."

"Except that never happened," he said, and I recognized the blank, confused look in his eyes.

It was the way people without keys looked after we talked about Hecate's Eternal Library in front of them.

But he'd remembered. It hadn't been for long, but I hadn't told him about us together in my room or in the cave. Those memories had been *his.*

And I refused to let him lose them.

So I kissed him again, moving closer this time, crawling onto his lap and wrapping my legs around his waist. His kisses became rougher, and with barely anything between us except our clothes, I felt him stiffen beneath me. I reached for the bottom of his shirt and pulled it off over his head, needing to be closer to him.

The closer we were, maybe the more he'd remember.

His hands traveled up under my shirt, my core warmed, and I removed my shirt so my skin pressed against his. I ground my hips against him, wanting *more.*

From the low, rumbling groan he let out, I knew he needed the same.

"Gemma," he said as I reached into his pants and held him firmly in my grasp. After all the months we'd been together, I knew the exact way to stroke him so he leaned his head back and shuddered with pleasure. "We've done this before," he said, and he pulled away, although his lips were inches from mine. "But this was where I always made you stop."

I nodded slowly, remembering all the other times things had gotten this heated between us.

You're going to make me lose control, he'd always said, and then he'd slip his fingers inside me, moving them expertly until relieving me of the pressure building up in my core.

From there, he'd excuse himself, then return once he calmed down, never letting me see him finish. He hadn't trusted himself to get past a certain point around me, and it had frustrated me to no end.

As if out of habit, his hand traveled down below my waist.

I craved the release he was offering. But I used my free hand to wrap my fingers around his wrist, stopping him.

"We're twin flames," I said. "You've had your first shift on Ember. We don't have to stop." I balanced myself on my knees and removed the rest of my clothes until I was naked in front of him. All I wore was the Holy Crown upon my head.

His pupils dilated as he drank me in. "It was you and me together all those months," he said, like he was in a trance. "It was never Mira."

He stared at me in wonder as I lowered myself to my knees and slid his pants off of him. Once he was freed from the remainder of his clothes, I crawled back up to face him, my knees on both sides of his waist, balanced on top of him so there were only centimeters between where he started and I began.

"Katherine used her gift to erase our memories," I said, quickly telling him everything I'd seen in the book. "That's what I just found out from Hecate. But we can complete our bond, and you'll get them back. Permanently."

I didn't know how I knew that.

I just *did*, with my entire heart and soul. Because Ethan was half of my soul. And once the bond was complete, he'd remember it all.

He *had* to.

He breathed slow and steady, like it was taking all of his effort to control himself. "Do you really think it will work?"

I lowered myself down more and grazed myself against the tip of him, teasing him.

From the fiery look in his eyes, he wasn't going to be able to hold out much longer.

"I love you," he said, and then he flipped me over, pinned me down, and slid himself inside me.

I gasped at the twinge of pain as he entered me, forever claiming me as his.

He groaned, a deep rumble in his chest, his eyes locked on mine. "Are you okay?" he asked.

The slight pain disappeared nearly as quickly as it had arrived, shut down by the fire burning inside me. "Yes," I said, and I pressed my hips up against his, my insides throbbing, needing more.

He nodded, satisfied. "I don't care how powerful Katherine is—I'll never forget our past ever again," he said. "I swear it."

Neither of us said any more, no longer needing to speak with words as we moved together, losing ourselves in each other until the world shook and exploded around us, sealing our twin flame bond forever.

39

GEMMA

"The last time I did a tarot reading, I learned that all four Queens would eventually rise," Skylar said to the group of us gathered around the round table in Avalon's meeting room.

The same round table where King Arthur had sat with his knights.

I still had trouble wrapping my head around that one.

Ethan sat next to me, holding my hand. He'd been like this since we'd made love three days ago—never wanting to break contact. It was like he thought that if he stopped touching me, he'd forget our true past.

We'd tested it out, so we knew he wouldn't. I'd been right that sealing our twin flame bond had brought his memories back for good.

The other Queens had been shocked after learning what Queen Katherine had done. A gift as strong as Katherine's wasn't one to be taken lightly. She could change everything we thought to be true, without us being any wiser.

In some ways, it wasn't much different from my own power. Except mine was more dangerous, since it could *actually* change the past, instead of making us believe that a different past had occurred.

Luckily, the others trusted me, because I was the fourth Holy Queen. Queen Katherine was a different matter. But we were going to discuss how to move forward with making an alliance with her later.

Right now our biggest focus was on Skylar, and on why she'd called this meeting. She sat at the seat in front of the fireplace, and the other Queens and I sat around her, with our mates by our sides.

Annika and Jacen looked far more at peace than they had when I'd met them in Avalon. Even though they were immortal, the grief that had been lifted from their souls made them appear years younger. I didn't think Selena had told them that she'd died in the original timeline, and I didn't think she intended to tell them.

Annika and Jacen would never know the lengths I'd gone to save their daughter. Which was what using my ability would be like—changing lives for the better, without most people knowing that anything had ever been different.

I was a hero in the shadows. And given that I'd never liked being the center of attention, I was totally fine with that.

Raven sat on the other side of her mother, with Noah next to her. The two of them were wildness personified, alert and ready to fight at a moment's notice. I barely knew Noah, and given that he seemed to be the silent, broody type, it might take him a bit to warm up to me, if he ever did at all. Raven's outspoken nature balanced his more reserved one perfectly.

Selena and Julian sat between me and her parents. Selena's magic was so strong that it hummed through the room, like constant noise in the background. She fidgeted in her chair, apparently anxious for the meeting to start. Julian, on the other hand, was still and alert, hyperaware of everything happening around him.

Skylar sorted through her tarot deck and pulled out four cards.

The Queen of Cups, the Queen of Swords, the Queen of Wands, and the Queen of Pentacles. She laid them down in a line, in that order—the order that we'd risen. In my card—the Queen of Pentacles—a woman sat in front of a tree, holding a staff with a pentacle on it, with crystals growing out of the ground around her.

"These were the first four cards I picked in that tarot reading all those years ago," she said. "But there was a fifth card above them—the Unknown Card. Now that the four of you have claimed your positions as Queens, I feel that having your energy with me in this room will be the catalyst to get that fifth card to reveal itself."

She shuffled the cards a few times, then fanned them out in front of her. She took a deep breath, closed her eyes, and picked one from the center.

She opened her eyes, flipped it over, and sucked in a startled breath at the image of a naked woman sitting in front of a tree, holding a bright red apple.

She placed it in its spot above the Four Queens, and I leaned forward to see the words on the bottom.

The Devil.

The woman painted on the card had features similar to Lilith's.

This couldn't be good.

I looked at Skylar, ready for an explanation. But she was staring at the card, lost in a trance. Because when Skylar did a tarot reading, she didn't just glance at the cards. They transformed for her, and she saw *into* them. It was like she was watching a movie that only she could see.

Raven observed her mom, like she was searching for signs in her expression about what she might be seeing. Annika was as calm as ever. Selena continued to fidget, only calming when Julian reached for her hand.

I was so focused on trying not to ruin Skylar's concentration that I could barely breathe.

When Skylar finally looked back up, her green eyes were dark and haunted.

"What is it?" Raven asked.

"The cards have shown me what Lilith has been working toward this entire time. Her end goal," she said. "And it turns out that she isn't the worst we have to fear."

My heart dropped. Because Annika and all of the supernaturals on Avalon had been trying to stop Lilith since I was a baby. If there was someone out there who was more dangerous than she was, how were we supposed to have a fighting chance?

This is why you needed to save Selena, I reminded myself. *The four Queens together are stronger than we could ever be apart.*

"Who could be worse than Lilith?" Annika's question echoed my thoughts.

"Have you met the gods?" Selena asked. "Because they're pretty damn powerful."

"They're also not trying to exterminate or enslave everyone on the planet," Annika said, so focused on

Skylar that she barely spared Selena a glance. "Tell us what you saw."

"Lilith has been gathering blood," she started. "Lots and lots of blood."

We already knew this, since the demons had been kidnapping gifted humans for years. They strengthened them, turned them into gifted vampires, then drained their blood. Figuring out the locations of these bunkers, rescuing the humans, and slaying the demons who'd taken them had been one of the Nephilim army's primary goals.

"We know this," Raven said impatiently. "Did you see *why* they're gathering the blood?"

"I did."

"And...?"

"Lilith plans on unleashing the darkest force in the world. One that has been locked inside his own prison realm in Hell for millennia. She's found the location of the rift that leads to his realm, and is going to bathe it in gifted vampire blood. Then, with the help of Lavinia, this dark force will rise."

Shivers crawled up and down my arms. "What type of dark force?"

"The darkest one known to man," she said. "The King of the Demons—Lucifer himself."

I hope you enjoyed *The Dragon Scorned*! If so, make sure to leave a review on Amazon. The more positive reviews I have, the more motivated I am to write the next book faster!

A review for the first book in the series is the most helpful. Here's the link on Amazon where you can go to leave your review ➜ mybook.to/dragontwins

---

The next book in the series—*The Dragon Queen*—is out now!

Grab it now at:
mybook.to/dragonqueen

You can also turn the page to see the cover and description for *The Dragon Queen*.

THE DRAGON QUEEN

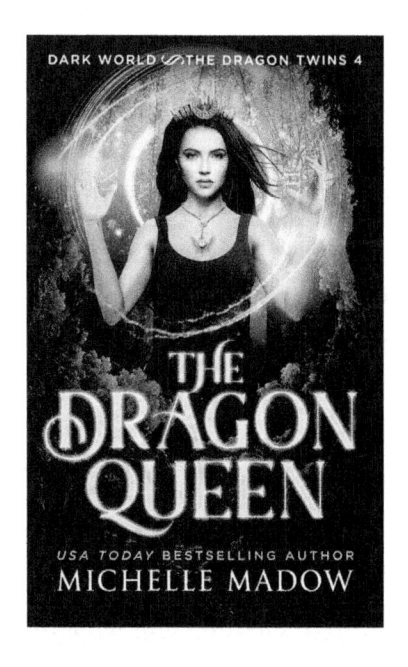

The final battle is here.

THE DRAGON QUEEN

Prepare yourself for a mind-bending adventure full of magic, romance, and twists you'll never see coming.

Gemma and her soulmate Ethan have remembered the true past they shared together. So everything in her life should be perfect. Right?

Wrong. Gemma's worst nightmare has come true. Her twin sister Mira has gone dark and joined forces with Lilith and the demons.

Gemma has already learned the hard way that she can't use her time travel magic to save her sister. But she *can* use it to help defeat the demons.

The best way to do that? Find the only Dark Weapon the demons don't have yet—the Dark Sword—and use it against them.

But the Dark Sword is lost in time—over a century in time, to be exact. Now, it's up to Gemma to find it and bring it to the present before Mira can get it first. And if Mira *does* find it first, Gemma will have to do everything she can to steal it from her, even if it means committing the ultimate act of betrayal: turning on her twin once and for all.

Hold on tight as you race through time with Gemma and Mira in the final book of the addicting *Dragon Twins* series by *USA Today* bestselling author Michelle Madow!

Grab it now at:
mybook.to/dragonqueen

Also, make sure you never miss a new release by signing up to get emails and/or texts when my books come out!

Sign up for emails: michellemadow.com/subscribe

Sign up for texts: michellemadow.com/texts

And if you want to hang out with me and other readers of my books, make sure to join my Facebook group: www.facebook.com/groups/michellemadow

Thanks for reading my books, and I look forward to chatting with you!

ABOUT THE AUTHOR

Michelle Madow is a USA Today bestselling author of fast-paced fantasy novels that will leave you turning the pages wanting more! Her books are full of magic, adventure, romance, and twists you'll never see coming.

Michelle grew up in Maryland, and now lives in Florida. She's loved reading for as long as she can remember. She wrote her first book in her junior year of college and hasn't stopped writing since! She also loves traveling, and has been to all seven continents. Someday, she hopes to travel the world for a year on a cruise ship.

Visit author.to/MichelleMadow to view a full list of Michelle's novels on Amazon.

THE DRAGON SCORNED

Published by Dreamscape Publishing

Copyright © 2021 Michelle Madow

ISBN: 9798744238131

This book is a work of fiction. Though some actual towns, cities, and locations may be mentioned, they are used in a fictitious manner and the events and occurrences were invented in the mind and imagination of the author. Any similarities of characters or names used within to any person past, present, or future is coincidental.

All rights reserved. No part of this book may be used or reproduced in any manner whatsoever without written permission from the author. Brief quotations may be embodied in critical articles or reviews.

❀ Created with Vellum